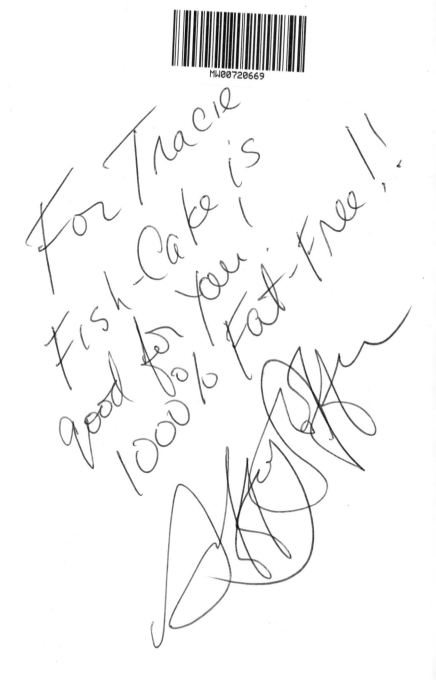

For Tracie
Fish-Cake is
good for you.
1000% Fat-Free!!

I'm Right Here, Fish-Cake

By
Jeffrey Shaffer

**Drawings by
Paul Hoffman**

CATBIRD PRESS

First edition

CATBIRD PRESS
16 Windsor Road, North Haven, CT 06473
800-360-2391; e-mail: catbird@pipeline.com
Our books are distributed by
Independent Publishers Group

To Max, Juanita, and Mif, a trio
who would have enjoyed this party.

Some of the selections in this book first appeared in slightly
different form in *The New Yorker* and in the Sunday
magazines of the *Detroit Free Press, Baltimore Sun,
Seattle Times,* and Portland *Oregonian*

Library of Congress Cataloging-in-Publication Data
Shaffer, Jeffrey, 1953-
I'm right here, Fish-Cake / by Jeffrey Shaffer ;
drawings by Paul Hoffman. — 1st ed.
A collection of short stories of humor, many of which
were previously published in various sources.
ISBN 0-945774-30-3 (trade paper : alk. paper)
1. American wit and humor. I. Hoffman, Paul, 1950-
II. Title.   PN6162.S49 1995
814'.54—dc20   95-15817 CIP

Contents

Over and Back

At first I didn't know what to make of it. "My God," I thought, "they've dropped The Bomb. After all these years it finally happened!" Then I realized that couldn't be true, since all the houses were still standing and I hadn't heard any explosion. But the streets were deserted, and there were no signs of life. It was, I should add, an absolutely beautiful day.

I turned away from the window and looked back at the bed. Empty! My wife was gone, too. Was this a perverse practical joke? How could everyone in Whispering Springs disappear while I was sleeping?

Then I saw a note lying on the dresser.

Dear Don:

I've made up my mind. I'm going with the others onboard the Mothership tonight. We've thought this over carefully. The visitors have been among us for some time now. My new mate is named Ixtl. He is a wonderful, caring, sensitive being. We will live peacefully in a world free from hate, envy, and the threat of nuclear war. There is a casserole in the freezer for you.

Dinuta

I took a shower and went down to the post office. Harold Squiegee was coming out the door. "They're gone!" I said. "The whole town!"

"Nah," he said. "There's a few left. I checked around this morning. Seems like they only took people who wanted to go."

"That's funny," I said. "Nobody ever even asked me. Do you suppose they could read our minds?"

"Reading our minds would certainly be better than watching us on TV all day," said Harold, gazing skyward with a philosophical expression.

Someone called for a meeting that night at the Black Cat Café to try and figure out what to do next. It seemed like our group should have a name, so we took a vote and called ourselves The Leftovers. I thought The Remainders was a better choice, more literary sounding, but nobody ever listens to me.

"We should have some t-shirts printed," said Cody Hopwell. "My wife could fix them up. We need to figure out a logo."

Curtis Suslaw pointed out that if we were all wearing club t-shirts around town, some stranger passing through would probably ask what The Leftovers were all about, and we'd really be in a pickle. Then somebody said it was almost time for *Murder, She Wrote*, so the meeting broke up.

I don't remember much about the next few days. I went shopping a couple of times. Hector Lasky was trying to run the Food-To-You all by himself, and a whole bunch of items were mismarked, so I really scored some bargains on Macaroni-Man Dinners and Mama Cheryl's Pocket Pizzas.

"Why do you think they left?" I asked him in the check-out line. "What's not to like about this place?"

"People always want something new," he said. "Men go out looking at fancy cars. Women go on diets. All I know is the weather there can't be as good as it is here."

It seemed like sooner or later the outside world would have to find out what had happened. My biggest fear was that one of Dinuta's huge, paleozoic brothers would get paroled and show up on the front porch. If anyone in her family got wind that she had disappeared without a trace, I could look forward to having my anatomy rearranged, with an emphasis on long-term pain.

And then, after about a week and a half, bingo! it was over. I woke up to the sound of a tea kettle whistling and ran downstairs. Dinuta was pouring hot water into a bowl of instant oat bran. She nodded as I came in.

"When did you get here?" I asked. "Is everybody back?"

"Yes, everyone. We got in this morning."

"Well, gosh," I said, "are you all right? Where exactly were you?"

"Can we not have this conversation," she said pointedly. "I'm really kind of emotionally spent. What I need right now is some quiet time."

They were all like that, short-tempered and surly, and it made things pretty awkward for the rest of us.

Harold Squiegee seemed to have a line on the situation. He told me that from what he could gather, the aliens blew the whistle on the deal almost from day one. Supposedly one of their scout ships discovered another civilization that looked more interesting than ours, and they decided to give Earth a rain check for the time being. The intergalactic "Don't call us, we'll call you" routine.

I bumped into Bud Yonkers a day or two later and tried to pump him for some details. "I'm just wondering," I said. "What was it like being on another planet?"

"Oh, so-so I guess," he said hesitantly. "The food was pretty dull. Well, I take that back. They had a nice pancake house, but I'm not much for eating out, you know that. And the weather here is a lot better, that's for sure."

9

Dinuta got crazy whenever I brought the subject up. But I really thought I had a right to be curious about a few things.

"Honey," I said one day as she was loading the dishwasher, "I don't want to pry, but I'm intrigued with this Ixtl person."

"What about him?" The tone in her voice hardened as she spoke.

"Well, what was he like? Did he satisfy you in ways I don't?"

"I knew it!" she said, flinging an imitation fiestaware cup into the top rack. "I thought maybe you'd wonder at the awe and mystery of a totally different race of beings, a lifestyle committed to the pursuit of knowledge and peace and universal understanding, but you're just fixated on the whole sex thing! That's all you ever think about!"

She packed up and left that night. I thought maybe she'd headed for the ozone again, but someone said they saw her in Halsey a couple of weeks back, so I guess she's staying with her parents down there.

I should hit the road myself. There's no one to hold me back now. I'll talk to a lawyer and then get moving. Well, maybe I'll wait a week. It's hard to just pull up stakes overnight. Also, I have to admit there are some good reasons to stick around. For one thing, the weather here is just so darn *nice* all the time.

Regular Update

To you, our dearest friend(s):

Happy holidays! Can you believe another twelve months have passed? Every year we keep promising ourselves that we'll write each one of you individually, and then we run out of time and have to send out this mass mailing. Hard to imagine how any family could be so darned busy, but keep reading and you'll see why we barely have a moment to eat or sleep around here!

First, about Krystal: as some of you already know, she was deeply hurt by the cancellation of *Full House*. When we try talking with her about it, the word "betrayal" comes up frequently. Plus, she's been very frustrated for quite some time by the inability of the networks to come up with a TV program that can harness the untapped potential of country superstar Garth Brooks.

To make a long story short, we agreed that she should take a few months off from the whole prime-time schedule and get in touch with her own feelings. She's been watching a lot of *Adam-12* and *CHiPs* re-runs each afternoon on our local independent station, and it's made her think seriously about maybe studying to get a driver's license. We also sent away for the home version of *The Price Is Right,* and that helped perk up her spirits. She'll be 29 next spring, so these little funks don't last as long as they used to, which is a good sign.

Scorpio has had quite a time. He's been canvasing the neighborhood gathering signatures on a petition to bring back *The Munsters*. Needless to say we were skeptical, except that he's researched it pretty thoroughly and says the key is to update the show and use its dark humor to confront serious issues such as political correctness, sexism, and drug legalization.

The surprising thing is that residents on our street have come out solidly in favor of the idea. Like most people, we've long accepted the conventional wisdom that TV comedies of the 60s were totally escapist and irrelevant to everyday life, but our young pollster may be onto something here that's eluded the big enchiladas. We'll see.

J.R. certainly is turning out to be a precocious little papoose. He got into a big tangle over the 6th grade spring history pageant and we had to file for a temporary injunction.

The kids were supposed to form small working groups and come up with short vignettes to illustrate significant events in our national heritage. Basically what happened was that the teacher tried to railroad J.R.'s group into a silly rendition of Babe Ruth's 60th home run. But we knew that idea simply had no room for plot flexibility or character conflict, and when we finally got into court, the judge agreed with us.

So J.R.'s group ended up performing their own original version of *Unsolved Mysteries* and it was the most riveting segment of the whole pageant. The only bad part was that it got sandwiched in between the bombing of Pearl Harbor and John Glenn's flight into space, but at least it gave J.R. a firsthand look at why a good time slot is so crucial in this world.

As for Marlena and me, well, being married means hanging on through the ups and the downs, and we have both had our share. There was a rocky period early in the year when she decided to start up a personal correspondence with Jacques Cousteau.

Her feeling is that the oceans are no longer the breakaway issue we need to galvanize world opinion toward a new environmental awareness in the 1990s, and she thinks it would be much more beneficial to put the old *Calypso* in dry dock and switch over to a rainforest preservation agenda.

So far, all we've gotten back is an autographed photo. As I see it, the guy is probably locked into a long-term development package with some stuffy network like PBS, and they don't want him to rock the boat. She's going to suggest that he cut a new deal with a hip outfit like the Discovery Channel or A&E.

We also had a really bad experience with one of those fly-by-night mail-order places. I can't believe we fell for it, but the guy on the phone claimed to have found a hidden stash of six "lost" episodes of *The Mod Squad* (including a supposedly original pilot version that featured Martin Milner, James Brolin, and Godfrey Cambridge as part of the team; the guy said they were all written out in later scripts), and the whole package was just $299 C.O.D.

The really painful part was that we had planned to use that money to upgrade the playback capability of our home video system so that we could output six channels at once instead of just three. The setup right now is still pretty crude. We miss at least two games each night during the NBA season, and it's a nightmare during the college playoffs.

But overall, we shouldn't complain too much. There's quite a bit to be thankful for right now. The Cold War is over and our country seems to be imbued with new sense of responsibility and accountability. Personally, I think this reflects a national trend that started gathering momentum during the last half of the 80s.

I was more than pleased when *Jake and the Fatman* proved it could pull down high ratings, although it didn't have quite the staying power I was hoping for. Still, I'm confident it will build a solid audience in syndication. And with the stunning success of productions such as *America's Most Wanted* and *Real Stories of the Highway Patrol*, it's clear to me that we'll never again have to put up with the kind of wishy-washy moral equivocation that was driven into our national psyche during all those seasons of *The Rockford Files*.

Well, time to get this in the mail. Hope you and yours had many rich, rewarding experiences such as the ones we've enjoyed this past year. Always remember that nothing is more important than making each day count. Marlena and I learned that the night we watched the final episode of *The Fugitive*. Ever since then, our goal as a family has been to strive for the feelings of happiness and personal validation that David Janssen's character, Dr. Richard Kimball, must have felt when he finally confronted the mysterious one-armed man who killed his wife.

Oh, one last thing: if anybody out there knows where we can get a good used satellite dish, please call us immediately. Our New Year's resolution is to double the number of channels coming into the house. If that happens, we may not have time to write at all next year. But stay tuned!

Sincerely,
The Uplinks

It Could Have Been

"Well, Brent, we're down to the final minute, with the Steelheads leading 20 to 6, and I'd have to say the turning point was in the third quarter when the Gigantics failed to score on fourth-and-goal from the one-yard line. That really killed their momentum."

"True enough, Irv, but a lot of people would argue that the real key to this game happened earlier in the week, when the Gigantics' quarterback, Steve Rubinski, won a Mr. Peanut lookalike contest and promptly announced that he was leaving the team to pursue a modeling career. His abilities are sorely missed, and team morale has been negatively impacted."

"Actually, Brent, I think the crucial factor today was a decision made last spring, when the Steelheads revamped their staff and hired Coach Shockley. Under his leadership, they're a totally different team than the one we saw last year.

"True again, Irv, and doubly impressive when you remember that Coach Shockley had no NFL experience and had just been fired from Aloha Tech after several of his players were implicated in that bizarre, 'sex-zombie' scandal. That tragic case of drugs, greed, and unrestrained passions changed the way an entire island felt about itself."

"And Brent, just a reminder for our viewers: tonight's Sunday Special Movie will feature a true account of that incredible incident and how it sent shock waves across college campuses all over America. Kate Jackson and Margot Kidder star in the network premiere of *My Sweet, Strange Kahuna*, immediately following your local news, except on the West Coast."

"Irv, I think our cameras are getting a good shot across the stadium right now—yes, there it is on the monitor. That's Seymour Champion, longtime owner of the Steelheads, enjoying the view from his luxury box, along with a familiar social companion, former U.N. Ambassador Jeanne Kirkpatrick, who, by the way, is intensely interested in football and sports physiology.

"And earlier this week, 'Sy' Champion told me that in analyzing any game involving his team, we can't ignore the importance of General Erich Ludendorff's final giant thrust along the Western Front of Europe in the summer of 1918."

"Brent, you raise an excellent point. As many fans may or may not be aware, Mr. Champion's grandfather was taken prisoner during that battle, and from his German captors he learned the traditional confectionery art known as *Mausenglage*, the delicate casting of fine chocolate into the shape of tiny rodents. This talent was, of course, the basis for the Champion Candy fortune that enabled the family to buy the Steelheads in 1934, when the team was about to go bankrupt."

"Irv, I understand we now have some news from our color analyst, Big John, who is standing by at the Steelheads' bench."

"Brent, I'm down here with noseguard Pookie Gibbons, who has played a heckuva game, guy's got blood all over his jersey, grass in his teeth, I mean hey, he's my kinda player! But ya know, in the off-season the Pook is no slouch either, we're talkin' Ph.D. candidate in Applied Geology here, and he just said that in lookin' at today's outcome we absolutely must keep in mind the fact that this whole area on which

Champion Stadium is located was at one time a vast alluvial plain.

"Massive beds of sand and gravel were extensively quarried during the industrial growth of the region, which later provided an excellent site for a sports complex. So you could reasonably say this game wouldn'ta even been played here this afternoon except for that quirk of natural history. Back up to you, Brent."

"John, you have hit on something that has come back to me over and over during today's game, and it has to do with the whole issue of time in the geological sense. I think back to that incredible period of some 20 million years ago when the earth's entire population of dinosaurs was completely wiped out by a process or an event that still hasn't been fully explained. And I wonder what would've happened if those creatures had survived, and progressed? Just imagine football as it might have developed among a race of huge, lumbering, intelligent animals, and it's fair to say the game as we know it would be totally different. Do you agree?"

"Aw, Brent, you know it definitely would be. I mean, jeez, you got a couple of big triceratops in the backfield can carry the ball, maybe a stegosaurus, you're talkin' eight, nine yards a crack easy, a whole different offensive game plan. In fact, the Gigantics coulda used some of that extra muscle out there today, the way they were gettin' shoved around by that big Steelhead defensive line.

"And Brent, if we're gonna look at key events, heck, go back even further and let's think about this whole Big Bang idea. I mean, here's this ball of molten gas and dirt and all kinda stuff just sittin' there and then *boom*! It's flyin' away in all directions and who knows where it's all gonna end up, I mean we wouldn't even be here on the air if that stuff hadn'ta come together just right. Ya ever think about that?"

"John, you're right on the money, as usual, and I think anybody who's been listening would be hard pressed to disprove the old saying that, in fact, this is indeed a game of inches. But we couldn't argue that point even if we wanted to, because the final gun has just sounded. This one is history."

Out of Order

In a study published in Friday's *Journal of the American Medical Association*, Michael Cosio of the Walter Reed Army Medical Center in Washington documented 11 deaths from falling soda machines . . . Survivors "made the same or similar statement about the descent of the machine," he wrote. "In essence, each victim said, 'It came down faster than I thought. I pushed up, but it was too heavy and it kept coming. I tried to get out of the way but it caught me.'"

—Associated Press, November 1988

I couldn't make change. That's how this whole nightmare started. Of course, that jerk was asking for trouble anyway. It says right on my sticker, "Insert Coins Slowly." That way I have time to scan the total cash input, calculate refunds if necessary, and then release the product.

But this hotshot came on like the 49ers running their two-minute drill, I mean he was pounding on the selection buttons before the last coin even fell into the collection box. And then the control circuits got confused, because they're wired to give immediate priority to the dispensing mechanism, even if it means disrupting the regular sequence.

So, *big surprise*, the main sensory panel skips past the change calculator and signals "Transaction Complete," and suddenly this walking meatball is in a rage, screaming and kicking me right above the coin return slot with the heel of his greasy Reeboks.

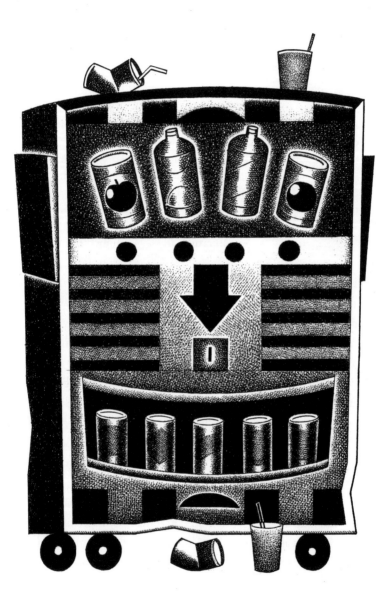

But I'm cool, okay? See, it was way after midnight, and I know from experience that's when things can get a little strange. People unload on me all the time, especially when they don't think anybody else is watching. And frankly, I can hardly feel anything with all this reinforced paneling and insulation inside the door. Most people get tired and just leave. I figured this loon would just follow the pattern. He caught me off guard, though, when he turned and went after Cubby.

I loved that little newsrack. He was chained to a lightpole over at the curb, and each afternoon when the *Post* came out we'd joke about the lurid headlines. Cubby was mechanically simple, but he was a class act. It really depressed him when people took extra copies without paying for them. "How can they think they're superior when they act like that?" he'd wonder out loud.

So when that slimeball threw Cubby down, something inside me snapped. He began to kick the little guy's clear plastic hood, and suddenly I felt myself charged with an incredible surge of energy.

Before I knew what was happening, I was right behind the moron, and as he looked back at me with a stunned expression I felt myself starting to . . . *descend.*

"You have to get out of here!" Cubby's squeaky voice was the first thing I heard when I came to. It was a dark and terrible scene.

"I . . . I was trying to help you," I said slowly.

"I know, but you've got to leave now," he said. "I heard footsteps. I think somebody saw us. Go quick. They won't try to blame it on me."

There was no turning back, that was obvious. My role as a quiet, reliable cog in the giant machine of commerce was over. I had become a fugitive.

For a while I spent some time near a candy shop in Brooklyn, hanging out with a cherubic gumball machine. Goober loved kids, and nothing made him happier than watching them lift the little metal door to see what flavor they had received. There was something pure and wonderful about their innocence.

It was a sentimental interlude that couldn't last. I was starting to run low on drinks. I knew that being empty would only lead to more trouble.

And then one day a punk with a long screwdriver tried to do a number on us. It was just after sundown when he ran up and started working on Goober. It didn't take long before nickels were spilling all over the sidewalk.

Then he put that piece of steel against me, and once again I felt myself being engulfed by an uncontrollable burst of energy, and things got very hazy. I was descending again, into that twilight world of chaos and broken values.

Goober didn't say a word when I came to. "It's okay," I said. "Nobody will hurt you now." But he was still frozen with fear, and suddenly I understood what he was really scared of. It was me. And I knew it was time to hit the road again.

A drifter's life is never predictable. Somehow I ended up doing a stint in the women's lounge at a theater somewhere along Broadway, and that's where I met Dagmar. She was from Sweden, and her dazzling chrome trim was the most lavish decorative design on any vending device I'd ever seen. Her face was dominated by a large panel of mirrored glass that was etched with scenes from the Arabian Nights, and her selection knobs offered a variety of elegantly wrapped chocolates and packs of imported cigarettes. I had no right to be in the same building with her.

The customers were like characters out of a dream, mostly refined ladies who treated us with respect and kindness. But, inevitably, the time came when my last beverage had been dispensed, and to stay on would have risked destroying the trust and goodwill we all shared.

I'll never forget my final night there. An older woman clad in a plush fur jacket put in her coins and then pushed every selection button, even the one for Diet Tropical Pow! I could feel the 'Make Another Selection' light blinking over and over, and I began to tense up, anticipating another ugly outburst. But then she just tapped me gently with her cigarette holder and said, "Not feeling well, are we?"

I headed south. Dagmar cried, but she'll get over it. I don't care what happens anymore. I just want to be left alone, but I know that's impossible. People see me and feel the need for quick gratification, and then they turn nasty when things don't go as planned. Why, I wonder, is humanity so unforgiving, so ruled by its primitive impulses? I guess I'll never know.

Your Chance, Act Soon!

Matchbook covers used to alarm me. 'NEVER FINISH HIGH SCHOOL?' is a question that still raises hackles. The rejoinder on the inside, 'FINISH NOW AT HOME,' was a heart stopper. For me, finishing high school at high school was bad enough. Why would anyone want to bring it all home? Various scenarios staggered my imagination.

I could picture Julie Ann Clinkscale, class tease, having a field day sorting through my personal effects. The wrestling magazines and bottle cap collection would become malicious grist for her gang of social terrormongers.

Joe Boggs, adolescent thug-in-training, would take up permanent residence in the kitchen, guarding the refrigerator like a Hun. I'd be lucky to scrounge some leftover sardines for breakfast each day.

Football practice on the front lawn was an idea almost too incredible to contemplate. It's doubtful that a single blade of grass would have survived. Even more disturbing was the notion of forty sweaty bodies trying to shower in our two bathrooms. 'FINISH NOW AT HOME' my rear end!

It took years to discover I had it all backwards. The circus aspects of teenage academia might have been avoided with the matchbook offer. Now I feel cheated. My diploma came the hard way.

What's worse, I realized, is that a brilliant concept is still crying out for innovative exploitation. Even now, large segments of our population are missing out on crucial, life-expanding opportunities. Common obstacles to leading a more complete existence include such drab duties as holding a job, raising children, raking leaves, and scrubbing bathroom fixtures.

But now, IN YOUR HOME, anything is possible!

The following is only the first part of an extensive network now being developed under my personal supervision: The Matchbook Life Enrichment Series. Soon all limits on worldly experience will be determined only by the number of surplus waking hours you have each week.

- **Military Training**. Never finish the Army? Send now for complete brochure. Programs available for each service branch, basic training to advanced field maneuvers. Boot camp exercises, recipes for combat rations, and personal weaponry all included in weekly shipments sent C.O.D. Note: Navy course unavailable in Iowa and Nebraska.

- **Professional Football Quarterbacking**. The dream of every red-blooded American! Materials include rope/old tire combo for passing drills (you supply tree), encyclopedia of plays and formations, plus tools for making tackling dummies from living room furniture. Practice signal-calling at your leisure, in the shower or driving to work. Supplemental guidebooks also available covering press relations and nightclub ownership.

- **Ascetic Lifestyle**. Meditate on universal truths within your own four walls. Simple blueprints and wiring charts tell how to disconnect phone, water, electricity, and other intrusions of modern society. Candles, prayer rug, and sound insulation panels all provided. Hair shirt optional. Learn preparation of cold water baths, standing barefoot in ice or snow, and survival on diet of rice and stove-top stuffing mix. Endure deprivation at your own pace, without embarrassment.

- **Touring the World.** Jet lag, lost baggage, rude waiters, and other travel irritations all avoided. Patio decorations provide realistic settings for each country "visited." Packet of metal slugs feel like foreign coins in your pocket. Also included are special capsules of water-borne bacterial organisms—YOU decide when to contract *turista* on this trip.

- **Running for Office.** Learn secrets of candidacy filing, campaign financing, and generating mass voter appeal without approaching any of the great unwashed. Evenings and weekends are perfect times to seek elected positions. Course provides important tips on direct phone solicitation, press conferencing via satellite, and the fine points of running rumor mills and whispering campaigns. Be President without giving up your current job!

The Matchbook Life Enrichment Series presents a cornucopia of opportunity. Untold benefits are yours in a low-risk environment. Gift enrollments for friends and relatives are always welcomed.

Your future is now! Close cover before striking while the iron is hot!

Home for Christmas

"Home for the holidays again?"

The cab driver knows me. It's a small town. At my destination, he stops in the middle of the street and flings my luggage toward the sidewalk.

"Sure you won't come in and see the folks?" I say, but all I hear is "Ho, ho, ho!" as he roars away.

Sparkling in the morning chill, the old front porch awaits me, covered by a fresh layer of white winter fluffiness. The creamy vanilla frosting is my mother's own special recipe, lovingly applied with bold, sweeping strokes that crisscross the floorboards and handrails with a series of interlocking peaks and valleys.

The buttery-smooth layers give way easily beneath my shoes as I walk up the front steps. After dinner, my young cousins will be turned loose on this area, and by the end of the night they will have licked every square inch back down to the finish.

A crowd gathers in the front hallway as I take off my coat and set down my suitcase. "Welcome back, Josh," says Aunt Gloria, leaning forward to give me a kiss. She is wearing a Santa Claus hat and a bushy white beard, and as her lips touch my cheek I suddenly realize that the beard is real.

Gloria is an actress, and has always stressed the importance of total commitment to each and every role in her career. "Listen," she says in an urgent whisper, "this character is incredibly complex, *and he's not a nice man at all.* Promise you'll talk to me later—okay?" I nod, and she grins and pinches my ear.

I stroll through the old house and feel the familiar, warming glow of expectation. How sweet it is that so little seems to change from year to year. At the end of the downstairs hallway there are rumblings behind the kitchen door. Can it be?

I peek inside, and a blast of steamy heat takes my breath away momentarily. Yes, as is customary in this house at this time of year, the configuration of the kitchen furniture, the counters, the stove, and the appliances, has been temporarily modified into an Indian longhouse for the preparation of the holiday dinner.

Many years ago, our domestic assistant, Mrs. Koslowski, attended a class in Native American Cooking and decided we should make this day into a celebration of multicultural understanding. She changed her legal name to Harriet Ten Feathers, and now, staring through the opening in the doorway, I can see her tenderizing the turkey with vigorous blows from a hand-chiseled obsidian tomahawk.

On the floor lies a sheepskin poultice she has prepared for wrapping the bird, along with a special blend of herbal seasonings. Harriet refers to this procedure as Tualit Keena-Ho, the Feast of Rainbow Warriors. Back in college, I once repeated the phrase to a linguistics professor, and he said it's more of a slang term that translates literally as "I am sweating and my pants hurt."

In the den, Uncle Elmore lies motionless beneath a single, glistening, two-hundred-pound Comice pear, the pride of this year's Harry & David catalogue. His efforts to incorporate the impressive specimen into the centerpiece of our dining-room table are part of his own personal ritual called Raising the Fruit.

"Hiya, sport!" he calls out cheerily. "Don't come in—I can handle this baby, once my second wind kicks in." In truth, Elmore has not gone unassisted for years. This harmless pretense helps him maintain the illusion of youthful vitality. I smile and say nothing. Later he will quietly lose consciousness.

In the dining room, my father is working feverishly to complete his own contribution to the festivities. The table is immaculate. Silver place settings and crystal goblets sparkle like treasure. In one corner of the room is a fifty-five-gallon plastic drum, exuding a savory holiday aroma. Since before dawn, my father has been carefully blending bread crumbs, wild rice, spices, and chicken broth in it, on a scale unheard of in most civilized countries. Before my arrival, he began warming the drum with a hand-held microwave generator until its contents reached just the proper combination of firmness and consistency. Now, before my again astonished eyes, rests the outcome of his self-taught culinary and sculpting talents. It is a minutely detailed full-size replica of the original La-Z-Boy recliner. In our family it is simply called the Overstuffed Chair.

Before sounding the dinner bell, my father gestures toward his creation. Tears prickle my eyes, and for a moment I am too overcome to respond. This is a Christmas honor usually reserved for special guests. Taking my hand, he urges me forward and then helps me ease down, so that my body conforms intimately with the contours of the recliner. A profound sense of total unity with all living things engulfs me as wisps of steam rise from the armrests, and every fibre of my clothing and my being is penetrated by the warm, oozing juices.

"Happy holidays, Josh. We've missed you."

"My sentiments, exactly."

"Here's something else," my father says, handing me a length of nylon rope. I can see that the other end is attached to a trapdoor in the ceiling. The old man leans close, and his lips form the word "gravy."

"Dad," I say, "it's great to be home."

What Can I Tell You?

My name is Weeb Hunnecutt, and I am an apathetic. It's not easy to talk about, even though I'm now on the road to a healthy recovery. Perhaps my story will awaken others to the danger of this subtle but virulent affliction.

I had no idea anything was wrong during my slide into the pit of generalized indifference. Thank God for my loving family. They saw what I was doing to myself, and forced me to deal with it.

The intervention happened on a Sunday afternoon last September, exactly one year after my retirement from the hardware store. I was sitting in the living room, examining my modest silver dollar collection. The house was so quiet that I dozed off. Suddenly, the TV set came on with a roar. A football play-by-play announcer started yelling at the top of his lungs. Then I saw my wife's younger sister, Murine, standing next to my chair. She was holding the remote control clicker.

"So," she said, turning down the volume, "how 'bout those 49ers? Think they'll go all the way this year?"

"Oh, maybe," I said. "Hard to predict that stuff."

"Weeb!" said her husband, Val, who was crouching on the other side of my chair with his face only inches away. "Don't you feel," he continued, "it's time for the NCAA to have a playoff system for Division 1-A football? Good idea?"

"I dunno," I said. "Seems like they're doing okay now."

Murine clicked off the TV. I looked around and saw that a number of my friends and relatives had gathered in the room, along with several people I didn't recognize at all. Their faces were all very stern and serious.

"Uncle Weeb," said my nephew Klaxton, "you can't go on like this. We're not going to stand by and watch you fade away."

"What are you talking about?" I said.

"You really don't get it, do you?" said Murine. "Weeb, wake up and smell the dog-doo. It's time to confront your total, all-encompassing lack of interest in the critical issues, ideas, and personal choices that confront every American on a daily basis!"

Then she held up some slips of paper.

"These are receipts from the Grocery Wherehouse," Murine said. "Right at the top of each one it says, 'How are we doing? Contact store director Janice Sikorski with suggestions or comments at 221-8124.' Weeb, have you ever called Janice?"

"Can't say that I have, but I'm not really sure," I answered.

"No," snapped Murine. "The answer is no. And if you don't believe me, you can ask Janice, because she's standing right over there beside the piano." I looked toward the baby Steinway and saw a perky blonde woman in a green polyester jumpsuit. She waved at me but did not smile.

"Mr. Hunnecutt," she said, "our records show that you are the only customer within a seven-mile radius of the store who has never given us any feedback about our service or merchandise."

"Same here!" said a wiry little man in dirty brown coveralls. He looked vaguely familiar. "I'm Hollis Bentsen, service manager at Central City Tires. We keep sending you reminders every 5,000 miles to come in for your free rotation, but nothing happens. Did we do something to offend you?"

"I know this is difficult, Weeb," said Murine, "but your pattern of unresponsiveness has become notorious around town. Don't you realize how much time and energy has been spent during the past twenty years to develop and implement new techniques for probing, tabulating, and analyzing the nuances of public opinions and attitudes? We're an interactive society now, but you adamantly refuse to plug in."

"Murine," I said, "this is very bizarre, quite frankly. If I have a problem as serious as you seem to think it is, wouldn't somebody have mentioned it to me before now?"

"That's partly our fault," said Val, rather sheepishly. "Some of us have been trying to cover up for you, Weeb. When you kept ignoring all the warranty cards and the service rating questionnaires, I started filling them out. On the card from your last visit to BoBo's Bar-B-Que, I rated the beef brisket as 'Hot Dang,' the pork loin sandwich as 'Jim Dandy,' and the overall cleanliness of the dining area as 'Spit 'n Polished.'"

"I'm guilty, too," Klaxton said. "When you bought that Disney home video of sing-along songs, I pulled the reply form out of the wastebasket and sent it back. I checked off the box that said you learned about the video from a 'trusted friend or relative.' And I also indicated that you purchased the item because you thought it was 'wholesome, top quality, uplifting entertainment for the entire family.'"

"We made a mistake," said Val. "I finally realized we were becoming part of the problem, not the solution." He paused, reached into his jacket pocket, and took out a small stack of postcards and various envelopes. "Can't you understand," he said, "that each of these unanswered rating cards represents a human being, a person seeking to connect with your feelings? Like this one from the Cozy-6 Motel at Dinky Creek. The owner there will never know if the best word to describe your visit would be 'restful,' 'invigorating,' or 'illuminating.'"

"It was just a regular old motel," I said. "I mean, if it'd been a urine-soaked hovel I might've said something, sure. Really now, how much am I supposed to care about a 12-by-12-foot room?"

"Weeb!" said Murine angrily. "That's the whole point. It's all well and good not to care about something. But there's no excuse for *not having an opinion!*"

"I do have opinions!" I retorted. "For one thing, I believe this gathering is totally ridiculous and completely unnecessary. What do you say to that?"

"Weeb! Weeb!" said Val, shaking his head vigorously. "You're in denial! That doesn't count!"

"Does my wife know what you people are doing?" I asked. "Where is Zona, anyway?"

"I'm right here, fish-cake," said my wife, stepping out from the kitchen. I knew she was nervous because that's when she starts calling me by little pet names, mostly food related. "I'm sorry, cheese-log," she continued, "but I had to do something."

"Zona is the one who arranged for this," said Murine.

"I was desperate," Zona said. "It seems like you're disconnecting from the world. Time after time I've begged you to participate in the Channel 3 News Telepoll, but you ignore me. You wouldn't even call in last week when they asked, 'Is life worth living?' We have a hundred and sixty-seven channels on the cable now, but you just putter around, looking at

34

coins and reading maritime novels from Naval Institute Press."

"Am I missing something?" I asked. "How can I be in so much trouble for minding my own business and not bothering anybody?"

"You've got to open up, scooter-pie, and express your feelings! How can our leaders in business, politics, entertainment, and the sports world make this country a better place if we don't tell them what we want?"

"Look," I said, feeling fatigued, "if someone really wants to know what I think, why don't *they* just call *me*?"

"Oh, but they *do*!" Zona shot back. "Nearly every day. Calls from Time/CNN, ABC/Washington Post, The Roper Group, they ask for you and I hand you the phone, and you listen for one second, and then you tell them 'No thanks' and hang up!"

"Oh, Lord!" I said, as the shock of realization hit me. "Are you talking about those young people who have names like Heather or Courtney or Logan?" She nodded. "Well," I said, sighing, "they're so darn pleasant that I just assume they want to sell me something, so I cut them off as quickly as I can get a word in edgewise. And it doesn't help that they always call right when we're having dinner!" Zona wasn't swayed.

"I was like Val," she said. "I lied for you, said you were ill, or on a trip, anything but the truth. Then, last Tuesday, Krista from Louis Harris & Associates called, and I told her you had lost your voice but could signal your responses to me in sign language. And then, once she started asking the questions, I fell completely apart. Should 'health' or 'wellness' be considered basic rights for Americans? Did the results of the last election make you feel 'angry' or 'ambivalent'? Are taxes now 'somewhat burdensome' or 'about right'?

"Suddenly I realized I didn't have a clue about what you would have said! You're becoming a blank page to all of us. And the only person who can change that. . ." her voice started to crack, "is you, pop-tart. Come back to us, please!"

Well, the sight of my dear wife quivering like a leaf was enough to convince me that something was dreadfully wrong. I stood up and held her in my arms while everyone in the room applauded and cheered, and then Val led me out to his pickup and we drove straight to the treatment center.

The staff was wonderful, sympathetic, and kind. My roommate was a well-known blues singer whose name I can't reveal for legal reasons. Like me, apathy had sneaked up on him.

"Everything seemed cool," he said. "Good money, easy livin', and all the while I was weaving a cocoon of blissful self-satisfaction. Fact is, I haven't written a new song in two years. The edge was gone. And baby, when you're a bluesman and you come to find out you don't give a rip about the basics—you know, lyin', cheatin', and drinkin'—well, you got no damn career left. So here I am."

Since my discharge from the clinic, life has been a daily whirlwind of surveys, interviews, queries, and evaluations. Zona can hardly get any time on the phone; the clinic notified the major polling organizations of my successful treatment, and now they're all calling me to get the opinions I never expressed during those lost years. I have also joined the advisory board for the Channel 3 News Telepoll.

Quite honestly, I have never felt better in my life. If you met me on the street today and said I look like a new person, I would agree. No, check that. I would *strongly* agree.

Worlds of Love

Slightly uncivilized SWM, poor (well, not quite) but handsome, smart and funny, eclectic and irreverent, fast driver seeks a lean, attractive to very attractive woman, 25-40, with intelligence, savvy and deep humor willing to go dutch in all respects into romance and supportive friendship. Film, Bartok to the blues, cafes, north coast, writers, tennis and understanding the Crab Nebula . . . does that help?

—Personal ad in *Willamette Week*

YOU: Spheroid, sensitive, methane-breathing, really a swell gal. Your visual acuity can pierce thick chemical atmosphere just as your perceptiveness can see past a limp opening line. ME: Oblong, athletic, semi-permeable membrane enclosing gelatinous crude-protein interior. A rare breed. Molecular simplicity doesn't mean we don't have complex emotional needs. Let's find the atomic structure of love. Reply Box X-15.

READY FOR SOME GANYMEDE AU GO-GO! Two petite, perky moon maidens enjoy low gravity, crystallized oxygen, Oprah Winfrey. Ideal respondents will be generous, electrically neutral, not intimidated by strong feminist outlooks or intense radio wave bombardment. Reply Box H_2SO_4.

BITE MY ARMS OFF! They grow back—really! Slim, attractive male, mid-thirties, crustacean background. Seeking active, aware female counterpart for quality-time relationship. Regenerative powers leave me incomplete without that special someone.

MACRENCEPHALIC AND MACHO. Cerebral mass accounts for sixty-one percent of body weight, just received real-estate license, ready for romance! Tiny pod feet mean limited mobility, no break dancing. If this brainy bonus package is for you, respond to Box Pi.

WHEN WE MEET there will be a *feeling*. When we touch there will be a *spark*. When we kiss there will be *combustion* at a thousand and sixteen degrees Kelvin. Are you a caring female type who combines lust for living with durable high-resilience outer coating? If so, we will share solitary strolls through searing underground caverns, enjoy loud hissing sounds, possible lava eating. Send photo and core sample to Box 10^{23}.

STAR WARRIOR. Hero of the Antares Campaign. Trained for conquest, now intrigued by the pleasures of power-sharing. Mountain biking looks groovy—can you show me where the pedals are? I like ladies who are trim, classy, open-minded, and can move quickly to avoid sudden, uncontrollable projection of razorlike claw appendages. Call Andromeda Exchange, ask for Eddie.

PARDON MY POLARITY. Cheerful, humor-loving, highly-magnetized male has Ursa Major needs for right date mate. Turn-ons include champagne brunches, home video, iron filings. Let's meet for some North-South sensuality.

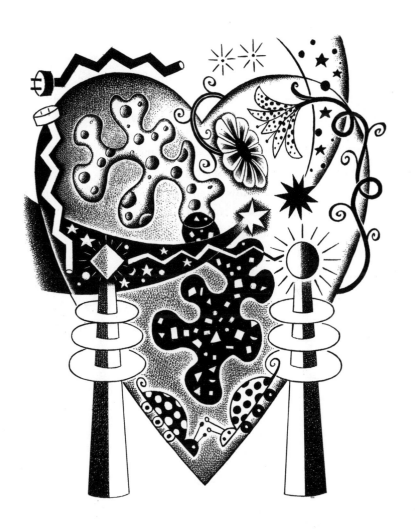

LIQUID LADY. Social life needs change of phase. Want responsible, financially secure male friend for possible long-term mix. You should be viscous, non-smoker, high surface tension a must. Shall we share a tall tumbler or a cozy carafe?

NOTHING LIKE SUN POWER. I open my leafy arms to reap the rays. My roots intermingle with the wholeness of humus. I feel the photosynthetic life force fill me. Every day is a journey of green grandeur. Chlorophyll is my co-pilot. If you'd like to ride along, contact Zona c/o this paper.

DESERT ROMEO. Not exactly handsome. Arid planetary conditions, fierce gravel storms take their toll. I am blocky, zero-moisture male, low to the ground. Friends cite resemblance to Roger Ebert covered with slag. Own and operate successful dry-cleaning business. Like to read, stand quietly, watch fungus. No airheads, please.

CYGNUS, do you read me? I'm sorry about what happened. Can we try again? Please realize that I have no way of knowing when you're upside down. Next time I'll be more careful. Call me. Bibi.

Where Does It Hurt?

One hundred hospitals, nursing homes and rehabilitation centers now contain realistic, life-size "villages," complete with cracked sidewalks, stores, automatic teller machines, buses, and other manifestations of modern life. There, patients can practice getting out of a wheelchair and into a car, going through a line with a walker, cashing a check and other everyday skills.
—*The Wall Street Journal*, January 1995

I had no inkling of trouble when the stocky, dour-looking man wearing a drab gray overcoat approached me on the sidewalk.

"You Doctor Grayson?" he asked in a raspy voice.

"Yes," I said. "What can I do for you?"

"I'm Detective Bates, Central Precinct, Bunko Division," he said, holding up a badge. "Come with me right away." He turned and began walking quickly toward the corner. "Are you the one who designed this place?" he said over his shoulder. "It's amazing."

"Yes," I said. "Recovery City is my creation. A fully functioning replica of an average downtown business district. My rehab patients get to confront everyday situations in a safe, controlled environment."

"Not so safe as you might think," he said. Rounding the corner, I looked ahead and felt a tingle of apprehension. Several people were standing together on the sidewalk outside the bank.

I recognized Nurse Olson, one of my top wellness counselors. Beside her was another man in a gray overcoat. They were talking with a woman in a wheelchair, Agnes Bloomfield. She was slumped over and appeared very upset.

"Dr. Grayson," Bates said, as we joined the group, "this is my partner, Detective Jeppsen. Mrs. Bloomfield has just been swindled right here in broad daylight."

"I feel so stupid!" said the frail but courageous woman. Agnes had been stricken with severe arthritis in her hips and was making slow but steady progress in learning to use a wheelchair.

"I was about to go into the bank here," she continued, pointing toward the heavy glass doors, "but then a man came up and told me he was the new branch manager. He said one of the tellers was cheating the customers and that I could help catch the culprit by withdrawing a thousand dollars from my account. Then they could compare my withdrawal to the teller's records and catch her red-handed. He was very convincing. But when I came back out here with the money, he just took it and walked away. That's when I realized it was all a hoax!" She began weeping again.

"Wait a second," I said. "This isn't a *real* bank, Mrs. Bloomfield. You know that." I looked at Detective Bates, puzzled. "Why would somebody pull a swindle just to get some fake money?"

"It has a certain logic," Bates said. "After all, con artists have been targeting senior citizens for decades. Now, with these new hi-tech rehabilitation centers opening up, it follows that grifters who are just starting out could use these facilities to practice their techniques before moving out into the real world."

"Or," Jeppsen added, "maybe some of the patients here are disabled con artists, and they're developing new scams to use on physically challenged victims."

"We've got to find out who else saw that phony bank manager," Bates said. "Jeppsen, see if the tellers have any information."

"Now that I think about it," Mrs. Bloomfield said, "a few days ago I was talking with Henrietta Barlow, that nice lady who had the bones in her ankles fused? She's on crutches, you know, but she started asking me a lot of questions about my wheelchair, and even wondered if she could try it out sometime. I bet she was planning to steal it right out from under my fanny!"

"Hold on!" I exclaimed. "I don't want everybody getting paranoid around here. The whole point of this facility is to build up people's self-confidence and trust."

"Doctor," Bates went on, "I want to speak with you privately."

"Fine," I said. "Nurse Olson, would you remain with Mrs. Bloomfield. She may need a sedative."

Bates and I walked a short distance away, and he put his hand on my shoulder, a more friendly gesture than I had anticipated.

"Doc, you may have dodged a bullet," he said in a low voice. "If the bad guys know we're onto their game, they probably won't bother you here anymore."

"What can I do to make sure they stay away?"

Bates took out a card and handed it to me. "Give us a half hour to get back to the station. Then call me, and I'll set up some work sessions to inform the patients about this new danger."

"That'd be wonderful," I said.

Jeppsen came back out of the bank shaking his head. "None of the tellers saw anything," he said. "The guy never went inside."

"Okay, let's head back," Bates said. "Doctor, I'll be expecting your call."

I spent the next few minutes talking with Mrs. Bloomfield in an effort to restore some of her damaged self-esteem. Then I looked at Nurse Olson and said, "Thanks for your help. And for calling the police. That was the right thing to do."

"I didn't call the police," she said. "I thought you did."

At that moment, the two volunteers acting as tellers in the bank came running out to the sidewalk, looking frantic.

"We've been robbed!" said one. "Somebody went through our purses and took our wallets!"

I reached down and grabbed my back pocket. "Good God, mine's gone too!"

"Those two policemen," Nurse Olson said, with a shocked expression. "They were crooks! It was all a big set-up!"

"Wait here," I said. "Everybody stay calm, and nobody move until I get back."

I took off running toward the administration building. But after rounding the first corner, I headed for the main parking lot, jumped in my car, and shoved the key into the ignition switch. However, before I could start the engine, my mobile phone started ringing. I picked it up and said, "Doctor Grayson speaking."

"You aren't a real doctor at all, are you?" said a familiar voice on the other end.

"Look, Bates, or whatever your name is," I said angrily, "I had a good thing going here. And now you've wrecked it all."

"So I'm right to assume you're not a licensed physician?"

"My wallet *is* somewhat incriminating!" I snapped.

"And it makes for great reading, too," Bates chuckled. "Four driver's licenses with different names on each one. But I'll tell you what really gave it away. All these screwball credit cards. No doctor would have a charge plate from Woolworth's. Or K-Mart. God, there's even a Diner's Club. Haven't seen that in years!"

"Does it really matter who I am?" I said. "Cripes, I was just trying to feed my family. Both of them. Look, what made you guys come nosing around my center, anyway? You sure went to a lot of trouble just to pick a few pockets."

"Actually, Doc, we were after you all the time. It's practically an open secret among the staff that you're a bigamist. I figured once we lifted your wallet and threatened to expose your double life to the public, you'd be good for some blackmail money. It didn't occur to me that you might be a medical fraud, too. That kind of blows my plan. I can't blackmail you if the police stumble onto your game and pull the plug on it. And they'll be buzzing around that place like hornets in a little while."

"Listen," I said, "maybe there's a way out. You give me back the wallets. I'll say I found them in the parking lot. Then, when things quiet down, we'll work out a payment schedule. That way, I can milk this operation a while longer and we'll all get something out of it."

"Sounds good," Bates said, "except for Nurse Olson. I've been living with her for the past couple of months. That's how we got the inside dope on your private life. Did you notice how she never made eye contact with me in there? She's probably sore as hell right now, since she's figured out I'm not a real cop."

"That does it," I said. "I'm heading for the airport."

"Wait a minute," Bates said. "Why don't ya come with us? We're heading east, and we could use a talented guy like you. Or," he added, with a harder tone in his voice, "we could just send your wallet to the police. So, whatta ya say?"

"Gosh, such a sweet deal," I replied sarcastically. "Where are you, anyway?"

"The aisle right in front of you, six cars to your left." I looked out the windshield and saw him waving. It took less than ten seconds to place myself in their front passenger seat. Bates and Jeppsen were in back.

"This is Moe," Bates said, pointing at the driver. "He played the bank manager."

Without warning, one of the back doors was flung open. Nurse Olson shoved Bates aside, jammed herself into the space beside him, and slammed the door shut.

"Get this bucket moving," she commanded. Moe, taken aback, started the engine immediately.

"What are you doing here?!" I asked, dumbfounded.

"I'm crazy!" she said. "Crazy in love with this big lug!" She grabbed Bates around the neck and kissed him passionately. Then she looked at me. "I knew you'd panic when you realized your wallet had been stolen and your secrets were in jeopardy," she said. "So I followed you. And thank goodness I did!"

"Nurse Olson," I said, "do you realize what you're getting into? You, a model care giver. And a regular church-goer, too."

46

"Boy," said Bates. "Nobody's ever fallen for me this hard."

"I can't help it," she panted, looking at Bates with undisguised lust. "You make me feel like a natural woman!"

"Hey Moe, you heard the lady. Get us out of here!" Bates ordered. I grabbed the arm rest on my door and held onto it tightly as the car lurched forward. The tires squealed from the sudden acceleration, and I smelled burning rubber.

"Geez!" Bates exclaimed. "I dunno quite where we'll end up, but it sure is gonna be a heck of an interesting ride."

"For once," I said, "I think you may be telling the truth."

In Play

It was going to be a perfect week. My son, Pericles, had received permission from his mother to spend all of spring break with me. I had cleared my personal calendar so there would be no interruptions and we would have total quality time together.

Early on Monday morning, his eight-year-old eyes were bulging in amazement as we examined a large bunion that had formed near the big toe on my left foot. "Does it hurt?" he asked as I covered the afflicted area with a medicated dressing.

"Yes," I said, not wanting to shield the lad from the hard realities of adult life. "It hurts like the dickens sometimes."

"What's it made of?" he said, with a tone that indicated the scientific interest of a possible future podiatrist.

Before I could answer, the doorbell rang. I told my son to remain in the bathroom, threw a robe over my pajamas, and hurried downstairs. Through the peephole in the front door, I saw my good friend Bubbie, who holds an important position with the local branch office of a distinguished and powerful investment firm. I opened the door.

"Listen!" he blurted out. "Something's happened. I was on a conference call with the big guys at the head office in New York a few minutes ago, you know, on my cell phone? And they were saying how lousy the market has been lately for buyouts and acquisitions. So I thought I would lighten up the mood, joke around a bit, and I mentioned your little operation."

"You told them about my clown business?" For the past several years I have made my living by performing in costume at children's birthday parties and other festive occasions.

"I'm sorry," he said, "I swear I was just kidding, but the next thing I knew they grabbed onto the idea like a school of hungry piranhas!"

"What are you saying?" I asked, genuinely puzzled.

"The point is," he said, "you're in play!"

He claimed that company rules forbade him to say anything else, and then ran to his car and drove off.

I had barely gotten the door closed when the telephone rang. The bunion was starting to throb as I walked into the kitchen and picked up the receiver.

"To whom am I speaking?" demanded a voice on the other end.

"This is Hanford Buelton," I replied. "Who's calling?"

"I represent Kellogg-Kronin-Powell, Incorporated, in New York," said the voice. "I am calling to confirm that you are licensed to do business as 'Boffo the Clown-tastic.'"

"I'm not sure I should be discussing my business affairs over the phone with a complete stranger," I said.

"This isn't a discussion," said the voice, "I'm just checking the data. It's also been brought to our attention that you've applied for three separate patents within the past year. Are those related to your clown activities?"

"If you must know," I said, "part of my act involves constructing humorous looking hats from balloons, and I'm trying to obtain patent rights for several original designs. My favorite is called DNA Disaster, and there's also—"

"I'll call you back if I need specifics," said the voice, cutting me short. "That's all for now."

My son walked into the kitchen and said, "Dad, can I see that thing on your foot again?"

"We have to leave the dressing on for twenty four hours," I replied. "How about some breakfast?"

"I want Funky Flakes. With chocolate milk on them."

"I might be out of those," I said, rummaging through one of the lower cabinets and mentally kicking myself for not remembering to buy his favorite cereal. "How about—?"

I was about to suggest a bowl of piping hot oat bran with brown sugar and raisins when I glanced out the window by the sink and saw a man unwinding a tape measure in the back yard.

"Stay here," I cautioned, stepping toward the door that leads to the side patio. The knob there is tricky, and I had to fumble with it for a moment before the door swung open. The stranger heard the noise and looked at me as I leaned out. He was writing something in a small notebook.

"Excuse me!" I yelled. "May I ask what you're doing?"

"Compiling the dimensions of the property," he said, holding up the tape measure. "It's part of the process for estimating your combined total asset value."

"Who gave you permission for this?" I demanded, and then the telephone started ringing again.

He reached into his jacket, took out a letter-sized envelope, and waved it at me. "It's all been cleared through proper channels," he smiled.

"Hey, Dad!" called my son from the kitchen, "Mom's on the phone for you."

My ex-wife, Paulette, only calls when she feels a problem is developing that could be my fault. True to form, she didn't waste any time with small talk.

"What's going on?" she snapped in her best accusatory tone. "Your name popped up on the financial channel a while ago, and Beaumont says there's a lot of 'buzz' on the street about a deal with K-K-P." Beaumont, her fiancé, was an aggressive commodities trader who once told me that greed is a function of biology, a natural craving much like thirst or hunger.

"No deals here," I said. "Someone seems to have started a wild rumor. I intend to scotch it."

"Just be aware," she said briskly, "that if your financial situation improves, we'll be renegotiating the child support payments. Is Perry all right?"

"Absolutely fine."

"Dad!" he suddenly yelled from the front hallway.

"Got to ring off now," I said, hanging up before she could prolong the exchange.

"Someone's at the door again!" Perry said excitedly. This time it was a tall, white-haired man wearing an expensive blue silk suit. He was holding a large manila file folder.

"I won't mince words," he said. "K-K-P is ready to make an opening offer." He tapped the folder and raised one eyebrow.

"I object to this!" I said, trying to sound intimidating. "What could you people possibly want with me, anyway?"

"Basically, everything," he said. "Real property, trademarks, all subsidiary rights to the 'Boffo' character, non-competition guarantee. You know the drill. Just initial the preliminary contracts I'm holding and it's a lock."

"Away with you!" I exclaimed, pointing toward the door. "There is nothing to talk about! Leave us alone." He didn't seem upset, or even surprised, by my outburst. However, as he turned to leave he kicked my foot by accident, and it felt as if someone had stuck the bunion with a hot poker.

The pain shot up to my ears with a ringing sensation, and then I realized the sound was actually the phone ringing again.

"Did you find out if we've got Funky Flakes?" asked Perry.

"Hold on, son," I gasped, limping back to the kitchen. A familiar voice was on the line when I picked up the receiver. "Things are suddenly looking very good," said Bubbie. "This deal could send all of us to the bank. My star at the company is rising by the minute."

"Don't get too smug," I said. "One of your stooges was just at my door with an offer, but I threw him out."

"Excellent!" he said. "The first proposal is always a smokescreen. Hang on now, and let the momentum build. They're talking about franchising possibilities, a Boffo cartoon series, foreign markets. Did you know that clowns are like gods in some parts of Malaysia? I could end up a vice-president if this plays out just right!"

There was a clicking sound on the line.

"Is that your call waiting signal or mine?" I asked.

"Must be you," he said. "I gotta run. Remember, play it cool. They'll sweeten the pot."

The waiting call was from my next-door neighbor. "Did you know there's a street vendor down on the corner selling items with your picture on them?" he asked.

"You're kidding, right?"

"I think you ought to check it out," he said. "Better hurry, though. The stuff was moving fast, and the guy didn't look like he was going to hang around."

I was almost to the sidewalk before I heard Perry calling, "Dad! Where are you going?" He was standing on the porch, scratching his head like a boy in a Norman Rockwell painting.

"Stay inside and lock the door!" I yelled. "I'll be right back. And don't answer the phone!"

There was no one on the corner when I got there. I did see a man across the street, loading a card table into a mini-van. "Hey!" I called, waving to him. He looked at me and shook his head.

"The clown stuff is all gone!" he yelled. "You need anything from Amway? Give ya a deal on the Zoom all-purpose cleaner!"

I memorized his license plate number and resolved to call my lawyer immediately. However, there was bedlam in the front yard when I got back. From a distance I saw Paulette and Beaumont ushering Perry into the back seat of their car. I tried walking faster, but the damn bunion felt like it was going to explode. And then I noticed two men dressed in blue coveralls standing off to one side of the porch. They were holding a portable drilling device that was noisily digging its way into the ground.

"I'm taking Perry home," his mother said, clearly irritated. "The situation is just too volatile. Not to mention the fact that he's here all alone, he hasn't had any breakfast yet, and you're running around the neighborhood in your bathrobe."

"G'bye dad!" Perry waved from the car. The boy is simply indefatigable. I waved back, trying not to show my anger. I knew it would be useless to argue.

"We may have to re-think this arrangement," Paulette said, slipping into the driver's seat. "I'll be in touch."

Beaumont took me aside and put his arm around my shoulder in an awkward attempt to appear sympathetic. "Listen," he said, "I know how you feel. If you ever need to just sound off about anything, don't hesitate. I'm here for you."

"Very charitable," I said.

"One more thing," he added, "I hear K-K-P may take your concept and go public with it. If that happens, could you possibly call and let me know what the IPO is going to be?"

As they drove away, I walked over to the two workmen.

"What in God's name are you doing?" I shouted over the noise of the machine.

"Core samples!" said one of the men. "Gotta make sure there's no underground contamination. The company doesn't want to get stuck with an EPA cleanup site."

Back upstairs, I pulled on a pair of pants just as the phone rang again. It was a financial writer who said he needed some background information about me for a profile article. I fumbled around for a few minutes, trying for succinct answers to his inquiries about how I developed Boffo. Then the bunion started to itch, and I became distracted as I bent over to rub my foot.

"Can I call you back?" I asked.

"No," he said. "I work for a national computer online service that sends my stories out while I'm writing them. It gives our subscribers a chance to experience the process of journalism as it happens. But I just have one more question on the human-interest side: What's your favorite food?"

"Why, uh," I was momentarily confounded. My mind had gone blank. "Cornuts," I said, for no particular reason.

"What?" His tone was skeptical. "Was that—*cornuts*?"

"Yes," I replied. He thanked me and hung up.

I finished getting dressed and slipped on a pair of fleece-lined moccasins so as not to irritate the bunion. Then, as I stood up, it dawned on me that everything outside was suddenly quiet. I looked out a window. There was no sign of the two drillers or their equipment.

The phone rang again. Bubbie's angry voice exploded out of the receiver. "Moron!" he screamed. "Were you born stupid, or do you work at it?"

"Have I done something wrong?"

"The deal's in the tank! That 'cornuts' quote spooked everybody in the New York office! They don't want any part of you now! What possessed you to say something so ridiculous? I may end up spending the rest of my career in the mailroom!"

"Bubbie," I said, "could we talk later? I haven't had time for breakfast today and I'm getting dizzy."

"Oh sure," he said, sarcastically, "have some breakfast. How about a nice big plate of cornuts? That sounds delicious!"

When he slammed down the receiver, the force of the impact made a sharp popping noise on my end. It sounded like someone had fired a small caliber pistol into the phone line.

Paulette brought my son back later in the day. "I've decided to give this one more try," she said. "But I'll be checking in every day. Try to get your act together."

"Everything will be fine, I assure you," I said, trying not to bite through my tongue.

"Beaumont says you really screwed the pooch on the K-K-P deal," she added. I just smiled tightly and shrugged.

The next morning, after we had each consumed large bowls of Funky Flakes saturated with chocolate milk, Pericles and I hurried to the upstairs bathroom. With the manner of a trained surgeon, I carefully removed the medicated dressing from my foot.

Both of us stared in amazement. A second, almost identical bunion had now appeared next to the first one.

"Time for a visit to the doctor," I said. "I can't tell if that thing is really a bunion anymore. It could be a car-bun-cle."

Perry patted my shoulder. "Dad," he said, "I like being with you, because it's always so interesting. I mean, Beaumont is nice, but nothing ever happens with him."

Holiday Season/Top
Individual Stats

Another incredible season is over, and it was characterized by several outstanding performances around the country. Long hours of practice and careful training led to these remarkable achievements. Congratulations to the following title winners:

RUSHING: Harriet Pringle, 58, Urbanville, Michigan.

Self-described "Granny à Go-Go" surprised friends, family, and pre-season pollsters by piling up 10,646 all-purpose yards en route to 177 separate purchases at 23 shopping venues. Though hampered by a deep thigh bruise suffered in a December 20th collision with a sales clerk near the cosmetics counter at the Drug Pipeline, Pringle maintained her frenetic pace until stores closed on Christmas Eve. Then, with only one day of rest and her left leg heavily taped, she locked up the title with a blistering round of gift returns and exchanges that included a spectacular early-morning dash of 256 yards across the main parking lot to be first in line at the customer service center at Mo' Better Mart.

PASSING: Leonides K. ("Sparks") Plugge, 41, Cornerstone, Maine.

Driving a battered 1971 Toyota Corolla sedan, Plugge used a combination of skill and stamina behind the wheel to pass a grand total of 1178 separate vehicles on assorted highways, back roads, and city streets without once being cited by law officers. Most of his forays across the center line occurred during a ski vacation at Vanilla Valley where, on successive days, his three children came down with mumps, chicken pox, and stomach flu.

Imbued with Yankee thriftiness, Plugge declined the services of the resort infirmary and instead chose to drive each of the stricken offspring all the way home, during some of the stormiest weather in state history, in order to receive free treatment from his brother, a licensed pediatrician. In the process he wore out six studded tires, three sets of chains, and four pairs of windshield wipers. The high point came on a lonely stretch of rural route J-15 southbound when Plugge swung out and thundered past a convoy of 47 National Guard trucks carrying emergency supplies to outlying farms that had been cut off by the storms. "That stripe in the road," he joked afterward, "it's just a guideline, not an edict."

RECEPTIONS: Lori-Ann Kreamer, 20, Dripping Springs, Oregon.

While most college students relax with their families during winter break, Kreamer (voted Miss Most Congenial in the 1992 Dairy Princess pageant) kept a smile on her face and a lilt in her voice during a whirlwind schedule of appearances at 217 different holiday get-togethers throughout the tri-county area. She was the featured guest at 16 tree trimmings, 11 caroling tours, and 17 eggnog socials, and also managed to squeeze in visits to cast parties for 13 different high school productions of *A Christmas Carol,* 10 junior college versions of the *Nutcracker,* and 12 community sing-alongs of Handel's *Messiah.* Kreamer says she averaged less than two hours of sleep each night during the season, "but I'll make it all up when I get back to my classes."

SCORING: Melanie Evelyn Bellows, 28, Delta Park, California.

Working as a charity bell ringer at the entrance to a discount food warehouse, Bellows received invitations for dates from 629 men during the course of her temporary employment. She accepted 327 of the offers and, as a result of those encounters, ended up receiving 214 gifts, including 21 silk scarves, 12 shetland wool sweaters, 26 pairs of athletic shoes, 17 lace slips from the Victoria's Secret catalogue, 11 strings of cultured pearls, 19 bottles of Obsession perfume, plus coupons good for free guitar lessons and a complete certification program in scuba diving. There were also 17 proposals of marriage, four of which she is now seriously considering. "They were all perfect gentlemen," she says of the experience, "but I admit I'm choosy." Bellows says women should never be afraid to set their sights high when seeking company from the opposite sex, and claims her most enjoyable times have occurred while in the company of loan officers, policy analysts, and university presidents.

TOTAL OFFENSE: Kyle P. ("Stinky") Stanley, 47, Littledale, Iowa.

The only repeat winner from last season, Stanley's poor hygiene and obnoxious behavior resulted in a string of offensive incidents that alienated and offended his relatives, neighbors, and community leaders, and made his name a household word on radio talk shows throughout the corn belt. Although he neglected to buy any presents for his immediate family, Stanley did reward himself with a gift box of giant super-spicy beef sticks from Hoopy Farms and a case of Old Boffo Bavarian Ale, most of which was consumed loudly and voraciously in front of the TV set watching bowl games. He also heckled Santa Claus at three different malls, causing a total of 126 kids waiting in line to cry. Stanley took perverse pleasure in subjecting holiday movie goers to his peculiar body odor (described variously as "a burning catcher's mitt," "root beer in a cat box," and "really, really old hamburger") during the annual screening of *It's A Wonderful Life* at the Shriners Hall in Mason City. "He's just a vile person," says prominent merchant Lester Woodburn, who has spearheaded two unsuccessful petition drives to have Stanley declared a public nuisance. Some townspeople say the community cannot afford the negative publicity brought on by such a repulsive personality. For his part, Stanley is already looking ahead to next season. "My goal for 1993 can be summed up in two little words," he chuckles. "Three peat."

The Great Leap Forward

"Mother of pearl!" I exclaimed. "It worked! We've traveled through time, Thurston!"

The acerbic tycoon fixed me with a stern expression. "That's *Mister* Thurston, young man," he admonished. Then he seemed to realize the significance of our achievement. "You may have just earned yourself a quick three million dollars," he added.

I knew Thurston was carrying a certified check in that amount as payment for my services. It was all quite incredible. Me, a swimming pool maintenance technician, crossing the final frontier with the richest man in Springdale.

It started almost as a dare. Thurston liked to sit beside the pool at his estate and complain about his boring life. "I've been everywhere!" he'd say. "There's no place that interests me in this world anymore. If someone would invent a time machine, I'd pay them a fortune and then I'd jump into the driver's seat!"

He didn't realize that I've always been adept at tinkering with electricity and small engines. I won't bore you with the technical stuff. To be honest, I'm not sure how I did it, but soon I got the right mix of magnetism, voltage, and radio waves. Since the gear was set up in my kitchen, I focused the energy output onto several small appliances. The results were startling.

I invited Thurston over for a firsthand demonstration, and he was impressed when I sent a food processor into the future and then brought it back with no ill effects.

"That's reassuring," he said. "I don't want this to be a one-way excursion." Luckily, he didn't know about the vintage toaster that I had sent out and failed to bring back. It was an unfortunate mishap; my mother gave me that toaster when I went off to Stanford, and it had a lot of sentimental value. Anyway, Thurston and I agreed on three million dollars as an acceptable fee, to be paid upon completion of the first journey.

The actual moment of time displacement was nothing more than a half-second of darkness, like the blink of an eye. We found ourselves standing in a room that appeared to be a parlor. It was decorated with elegant wooden antique furniture, and several large oil paintings of rustic farm scenes were hanging on the walls. The curtains were tightly drawn over all the windows.

"Did you send us backwards by accident?" Thurston asked. "This looks like a Victorian setting to me."

"They definitely have electricity," I said, pointing up to a brightly glowing brass fixture hanging from the ceiling.

Suddenly, a door opened and a man confronted us. He was wearing a plain blue suit, narrow black tie, wingtip shoes, and appeared to be in his middle sixties.

"I knew I heard voices," he said. "Are you ghostly spirits? This house is crawling with ghosts, but you don't look familiar."

"We're time travelers," I said. "We've come from the late 20th century. What year is it now?"

"Well, I'm not exactly sure," the man replied. He didn't seem to grasp the historic importance of our sudden appearance.

"How can you *not* know what *year* it is?" Thurston interjected. "That's simply preposterous!" I cringed, but the man remained curiously serene and unaffected by Thurston's bellicose attitude.

"Well, I realize this may come as a shock to you," the man said, "but the fact is, time has *stopped!*"

"Stopped?" I repeated. "You mean, everything has come to a halt? The sun is just stuck up in the sky all day long?"

"Oh, no," he said quickly. "Things are still in motion. We have day and night, that's no problem. But society has reached a sort of cultural equilibrium. Nothing is changing anymore, so people don't really keep of track of time very much."

"I should have known something like this would happen," Thurston lamented. "It's those damn Democrats, I suppose."

"Actually," said the man, "the trend was well underway by your time period. You probably only traveled a few years ahead."

"How do you figure that?" Thurston said.

"Think about it," said the man. "In the 1990s, kids were listening to the same kind of music as they did in the 1970s. The pace of change was slowing down considerably."

"You're right," I agreed. "In the 70s, none of us were listening to music from the 50s. It seemed really primitive."

"Exactly," said the man. "The same kind of social stagnation occurred everywhere. We reached the ultimate athletic records. There comes a time when a human body can't run any faster or pole vault any higher. So why bother going to a track meet?

"The space program got slashed because it cost too much to be sending people up there. And when the experts looked closely at the other planets, none of them really seemed worth exploring."

"So," I said, "all the great technological predictions for the future never came to pass? We never got cars that drive all by themselves, guided by a special cable buried in the pavement?"

"Boy, I remember hearing about that when I was a kid," the man said. "Nope. Never happened. In fact, finding a parking place downtown is still a problem that's never been solved.

"And even with all the cable channels we've got, the most popular TV show is still re-runs of *The Brady Bunch*. Frankly, I don't even know anyone who watches TV. I threw mine away."

"This is so strange," I said. "I always thought the future would look like *2001: A Space Odyssey*. With fancy robots and people dressing in spacey-looking clothes, stuff like that."

"Hah!" said the man. "The real 2001 looked just like 1988. As for my own clothes, I must confess that I'm using Richard Nixon as a role model. I've seen pictures of him wearing a plain blue suit around the house, and it turns out to be quite comfortable. It also takes the guesswork out of planning your daily wardrobe."

"Do you mind if we have a look outside?" Thurston asked. "I always like to see the landscape, the big picture."

"Certainly," said the man. "I'll show you to the front door, but I have to stay inside. My skin and eyes are very light-sensitive. That's why I keep the curtains drawn all the time."

He led us out of the room and into a long hallway. The front door of the house was visible at the far end of the hall. The wooden floor creaked loudly with each step we took. Rows of shelves covered each wall, and the shelves were all crammed with a vast assortment of odd bric-a-brac. When we were about halfway to the door, I noticed a familiar item.

"Hey, there's my toaster," I said. It was sandwiched between a chunk of quartz and a cookie jar replica of Cher's head.

"I'm afraid you're mistaken," said the man. "That is a heating unit from one of the early Apollo missions. It was given to me by my longtime friend, astronaut Donald 'Deke' Slayton."

"No way," I replied, reaching toward the shelf. I picked up the toaster and flipped it over. "See on the bottom here? I etched my name and driver's license number."

"Point of order," Thurston interrupted. He was now standing at the front door. "There's some mail on the floor. It must have come through the slot." He bent over to pick up the letters.

The man quickly took the toaster out of my hands, placed it back on the shelf, and pushed me toward Thurston. His face had assumed a curiously detached expression.

"Wait a second," Thurston said. "This letter is postmarked last Tuesday, and it's addressed to a Leonard Cooney on Emerald Avenue. *You* live on Emerald Avenue! What's going on here?!"

The man didn't answer. He grabbed the mail from Thurston, opened the front door, and roughly shoved us onto the porch. The door slammed, and Thurston looked out toward the street. My stomach was churning.

"There's my car right up the block!" he exclaimed. "For God's sake, we've been talking to one of your neighbors and you didn't even know it!"

"But I've never seen him face to face," I said. "Look, Mr. Thurston, that man in there is the neighborhood eccentric. We call him Cooney the Looney because he stays inside all the time with the curtains closed. It's been that way for as long as I've lived here. How could I know what the inside of his place looked like?"

"Stop the excuses," Thurston said, imperiously. "This trip wasn't worth two cents." He reached into his jacket pocket, took out the certified check, waved it in front of my face, and then tore it into small pieces.

"Wait a minute," I protested. "We just teleported ourselves through space. Doesn't that count for something?"

"I don't need a teleportation device!" he snapped. "I've told you before, there's no place I want to go these days. I should've known better. How could a pool man travel through time?"

He walked to his car and drove away. I got a letter the next day informing me that he was terminating the pool service contract. I couldn't get the device to work again, either. I tested it a couple of times, but nothing went anywhere. I don't know what changed, or how to correct it. The darn thing is sitting down in the basement for the time being. I'm going to check it once a month for a while. Maybe it'll fix itself.

Routine Stop

Suddenly, from out of nowhere, flashing red lights filled my rearview mirror. Puzzled, I swung over to the shoulder of the highway and rolled down my window as the tall, burly officer approached the car. He was holding a clipboard in one hand.

"Bob, we have to talk."

"You called me Bob," I said, "and I haven't even taken out my license yet."

"No need," he said, looking at the clipboard and flipping through the attached papers. "Robert C. Knudelblauer, Valley State, class of '75. Married, no children. Blond hair, blue eyes, six feet, 198 pounds. It's all in the database, Bob. I dialed in your plates on my CR-600K mobile terminal, nine miles back. I knew you had one continuous eyebrow before I even turned my lights on."

"Wait a minute," I said. "How is that possible?"

"Bob, we can access anything these days. Your NERD file is quite extensive."

"My what?!"

"Never Ending Regional Dossier. It's constantly updated by a consortium of 39 major credit unions, service organizations, and mail-order catalogue companies. I punch in the code and out comes the hard copy. For starters, I see you're late with this month's mortgage payment."

"Oh, I . . . that is . . . I mailed it yesterday. We had some other expenses I didn't plan on."

"Really?" said the officer. "I guess those three-day weekends at Beaver Lake Resort can add up pretty fast."

"Hey!" I said. "That's my personal business!"

"Bob, get with the program. Where do you suppose all those credit card receipts end up? The DREC system."

"DREC system?"

"Domestic Records on Every Consumer," he said. "Big center down in Florida. They can track down card numbers that haven't even been issued yet."

"But what's wrong with Beaver Lake Resort? Why can't I have a little break from the rat race now and then?"

"It's costing you an arm and a leg, that's why." He shuffled through the stack of papers again. "How come you gave up on Dusty Ed's Smokehouse Lodge? You stayed there every summer until four years ago. That place has reasonable rates."

"Well, you know, it seemed like the food was really going downhill."

"Oh Bob, that excuse is straight from Hooterville. You ought to just admit the place wasn't pricey enough. I notice you've been dining out at the Riviera Palace lately. I have to say they do a super job on the brook trout there."

"Never tried it."

"That's because you always go for the deluxe side of the menu, all that fancy stuff with sauce on it, like poached salmon. Joanne has the dinner salad."

"Leave my wife out of this!"

"No can do, Bob. She's already in it up to her mock-pearl necklace, the one you got on sale last Christmas at Bargain Barney's. Don't you notice a pattern here? While you're out tooling around in this spiffy new Lanzo Calzoni coupe, Joanne is stuck with a '68 wagon that violates every clean air standard in North America."

"Excuse me, Officer, but I'm feeling very confused and intimidated right now."

"Don't change the subject, Bob. When you hurt your neck at the athletic club last year, Joanne was the one who ended up paying the emotional freight and driving you back and forth to the chiropractor. Why'd you join that club, anyway?"

"I'm trying to stay in shape. Is that so unusual?"

"Well, according to this here, you've actually gained 15 pounds since you joined. Slimming down takes hard work. It won't happen in the jacuzzi, Bob, it just won't happen."

"Look," I said, "I don't think I have to put up with this."

"Oh, sure. You'd like to just peel out of here and leave this whole discussion in the past. That might've worked in college, Bob, but not here. This isn't History 117."

"History 117? But—"

"I know, Bob. The whole sorry mess is here in the FISH base. Final Intercollegiate School Histories. You gave Professor Blankenship a sob story during finals week about your dying grandmother. How many times did that poor woman pass away? I count five, but these records only go back to 1970. So you got to cool out for a whole semester writing a make-up paper on possible Navajo links to ancient astronauts."

"Hey, it was my Erich von Daniken period. All students go through that. Anyway, the prof gave me a B, so it couldn't have been that bad."

"So what you're saying is, the end is more important than the means."

"What I'm saying is, I'm not in college anymore. Maturity tends to broaden a person's outlook."

70

"Really? What about those orders from the Reader's Choice Club, you know, the deal where you get three hardcover editions for one dollar? Cough it up, Bob. You just want the freebie introductory specials. Once you get the bonus gift item, boom! You cancel your membership."

"So? It says I can do that right on the coupon."

He looked at the clipboard and shook his head. "Bob, we are not talking about the letter of the deal. Bob, we are talking about the spirit. You've been milking that introductory offer for donkeys' years. According to TRASH, Trends in American Spending Habits, 'R. C. Knudleblauer' got the teflon-coated pots and pans, 'Robert C. Knudleblauer' received the scratch-proof barbecue utensils, 'R. Clement Knudleblauer' got the Norman Rockwell decorator canisters, etcetera, etcetera. C'mon, Bob! Do you really think you're fooling anybody?"

"All right!" I snapped. "I get the point!"

"Actually, Bob, the few books you *did* order during the past few years make the point loud and clear. Early on, you were picking quality titles like *Heart Of Darkness*, *Atlas Shrugged*, and *The USA Trilogy*. But this last go-round, when 'Mr. Robbie Knudleblauer' signed up for the introductory offer, you opted for two Cajun cookbooks and a Garfield the Cat retrospective. Not good, Bob, not good at all."

"Please!" I said. "Can't you see that I'm visibly shaken? Why did you stop me, anyway? I'm sure I wasn't speeding."

"Bob, aren't you listening to me? This has nothing to do with your car. It's *you*, Bob. You've been going too fast for your own good all these years. I may regret it, but I'm going to let you off with just a warning this time. Slow it down, buddy. You stay in the hot lane and you'll hit the wall sooner or later. I'm just glad I caught up with you before it was too late."

"What should I do?"

"Step outside your own ego. Think about other people. Stay home tonight and reconsider your personal goals."

"But I have dinner reservations at the Riviera Palace."

"Not anymore," he said. "Joanne has canceled them by now. I talked to her on my cellular phone just before I pulled you over. She said this is the best thing that could've happened. Go home, Bob. She's waiting for you."

"Good Lord," I said, slumping forward onto the steering wheel. Drops of sweat stung my eyes like pepper. "I guess, well, I never really believed anybody cared about me until now. I owe you a debt of gratitude, Officer."

"Don't mention it, Bob. That's why we're here." He gave me a friendly cuff on the shoulder, and then turned and walked back to his car. The last I saw, he was skillfully maneuvering into the rush-hour traffic, on the lookout for someone else to serve and protect.

She's New!

MEMORANDUM

To: All Girls
From: HasBeen Toys, Inc.
Re: Buying Opportunity

I'm Jewel. I'm a one-toy extravaganza. I'm the only play-provider you will ever need again.

Like all modern women, my lifestyle is multifaceted. Sometimes I am Jewelyn Cassidy, powerful and respected corporate head of a high-boron diet-formula empire. But in between board meetings I become Jewel, glamorous fashion model and lithe, innovative inventor of Drivercise aerobic workout tape.

My boyfriend, Turk, comes with lap-top switchboard to screen phone calls, and quick-mix packets of Powdered Power Breakfast that blend instantly with your favorite beverage of choice. His thick, brush-cut hairstyle doubles as handy whisk broom to sweep up stray granules and minimize meal messiness.

When company complications build up and fuel my need for freedom, lock on Magic Hindquarters with Spinal Adapter (both sold separately) and I gallop into greener pastures as Homey Little Pony. Executive Garment Bag holds my halter-top/saddle spring fashion ensemble; I'm always ready for dress or dressage.

Unique modular design of my corporate cubicle work station allows for easy unfolding and reassembly into Pristine Paddock, where I am combed and curried by faithful Turk, a former Olympic modern-pentathlete who never suspects that his beautiful boss and four-legged riding partner are one and the same (by the way, men really are like this—it's astounding!).

For a leisurely lunch, Turk pampers me with steaming 10-grain mash; each portion comes in microwaveable plastic pouch, which slips easily into special-design Laura Ashley Action Nosebag that fits my busy schedule and petite equine jaw structure.

Sometimes I am threatened by menacing powers of Skele-Tron, enemy of balanced nutrition and mischievous promulgator of anorectic dietary misinformation. His brittle, bone-rattling presence requires immediate countermeasures.

Moving stirrups to forward position retracts my eyes into "vacant stare" setting and activates hydraulic linkage system to refillable containerized saddlebags. Squeezing bags with sudden force sends spectacular streams of BloodSlime SpookyGoo gushing from my eye sockets, guaranteed to gross out archrivals from any dimension.

Other affordable accessories help me transcend time and space. Ask store clerk to demonstrate Computer Companion Hitching Pad; Turk's riding crop snaps into place for use as omnidirectional joystick, while monofilament copper-stitching on my bridle and reins lets you connect directly into nearest video monitor for endless interactive entertainment.

Patented rabbit-ear signal splitter divides video screen in half to double-input capabilities, and isolates both brain hemispheres for added excitement.

When hunger pangs persist, I am transformed by miracle mixing blades into Ninja Whippy Yogurt Mutant. Contoured multi-speed control handle and self-defense recipe book are the secret to well-nourished personal security. Add pre-measured yeast syrup to equal parts of whole milk, and in minutes my gleaming chrome spigot rotates in any direction to dispense gobs of creamy dairy smooth goodness, or a kick to the groin.

Paper hat and stained apron switches Turk into the role of Jerk, expert soda fountain tender and sundae maker. His expression of vapid contentment lends continuity to the unexpected twists and turns of my high-energy agenda.

I am Jewel. I am happening. My hair is non-toxic. Best of all, I am now available somewhere near you.

Special Delivery

One cool autumn afternoon, a little boy named Jimmy Witherspoon walked out to the mailbox in front of his house. Jimmy enjoyed bringing in the cards, letters, and magazines that arrived each day. Being in charge of the mail was important.

But this time, something extraordinary happened. When Jimmy pulled open the door of the mailbox, he was startled to hear a small voice yell, "Hey! Who's there?" He looked inside and saw, huddled behind the stack of envelopes, a tiny man.

"I'm Jimmy," he said. "What are you doing in our mailbox?"

"I thought I would live here for a while," said the little man. "You may call me Mister Pilgrim. I have traveled across many frontiers in my life. Please forgive my tattered garments."

Mister Pilgrim had a scruffy beard and long, stringy hair. His clothes were badly wrinkled and smeared with dirt. He was sitting on what appeared to be a miniature sleeping bag.

"You look like Daniel Boone," said Jimmy. "He lived on the frontier, too. I read about him in school."

"I knew Daniel Boone well," said Mr. Pilgrim. "If you wish, I will tell you about him, and about all the famous people I have met. But you must promise not to mention any of this to your parents, or any grownups. It must be our secret."

"I promise," said Jimmy.

"Wonderful," said Mr. Pilgrim. "It's important to remember, Jimmy, that while your parents may truly love and care about you, deep inside they are really ignorant blockheads who enjoy pushing around people who are small and can't fight back."

"Gosh!" Jimmy exclaimed. "I've thought the same thing sometimes, but there's never been anybody I could tell."

"Well, run along now," said Mr. Pilgrim. Then he added, "Oh, and could you bring me some milk and cookies tomorrow? And an apple for dessert? My travels have left me very hungry."

Jimmy was happy to help his new friend. During the next few days, he searched the kitchen for special treats. Whenever he found something that Mr. Pilgrim had requested, he would carefully wrap it in a napkin and take it to the mailbox.

"You are a good scavenger," Mr. Pilgrim said. "That is a talent that can serve you well. Especially when society tries to crush your spirit, robs you of all opportunity to live with dignity, and then kicks you into the gutter like an old bone."

"Tell me about Daniel Boone," Jimmy said.

"Oh, he was quite a fellow," Mr. Pilgrim said. "But I'm rather tired right now. And it's best that your parents not see you lingering out here. I suggest that, from now on, you visit me late at night. Then we'll have privacy, and you'll gain strength and coordination by learning how to climb out of your bedroom window without waking anybody up."

It was indeed more fun talking with Mr. Pilgrim at night. He would sit at the front of the mailbox with his tiny legs dangling over the edge while the moonlight shone brightly on the long, wavy strands of his greasy beard. He told

Jimmy of many heroic events in which he had participated during his long life.

"Were you scared at the Alamo?" Jimmy asked.

"Yes, but I overcame the fear," Mr. Pilgrim said. "Remember, Jimmy, that if you believe in yourself there's no reason to be afraid. Still, the fact remains that most of your dreams and aspirations will always be unfulfilled, your best friends will turn out to be worthless frauds, and you'll spend a lot of time choking on the bitter tears of defeat."

"Sometimes I feel kind of bad about the things you tell me," Jimmy said. "Aren't there some good rules I should remember?"

"Oh, absolutely," said Mr. Pilgrim. "For one thing, never draw to an inside straight. And, equally important, never allow yourself to be caught in a public place without any pants."

One day Jimmy couldn't resist the urge to share his secret. His friend Lissa lived on the next block, and she did not believe Jimmy when he told her about the little man in the mailbox. But when Jimmy took Lissa to the box and tapped lightly on the side, nothing happened.

"Mr. Pilgrim?" he asked, opening the door. "I want you to meet my friend Lissa." It looked like the tiny sleeping bag was bunched up in a back corner. Jimmy thought Mr. Pilgrim might be hiding underneath it. But before he could reach in to search around with his hand, a mail delivery truck appeared at the end of the block and he quickly closed the box so the mailman wouldn't become suspicious. Lissa got bored and walked home.

"I'm sorry if you were embarrassed," Mr. Pilgrim said, later that night. "I just didn't feel well this afternoon when you came knocking. That's why I didn't answer."

"Now Lissa thinks I'm a dope," Jimmy said, sadly.

"Jimmy, here is more important advice: Don't fall for the first skirt that goes by. And remember that girls are like trains. If you miss one, just keep waiting and pretty soon another will show up. Also, here are two words that will save you a lot of money: Dutch treat."

"Mr. Pilgrim," Jimmy said, "will you always be around to talk to me about these things?"

"Well, that all depends," said the little man, smiling. "There is one thing that would help me stay a bit longer. I want you to go into your dad's den and look in that cabinet where he keeps the drinks that are just for grownups. You'll see a tall, triangular-shaped green bottle that says 'Glenfiddich' on the label. Please pour some into a large cup and bring it to me."

"How do you know where all that stuff is?" Jimmy wondered.

"Oh, I've done a little scouting while you were at school and the folks were at work. Kit Carson taught me a few tricks about that kind of thing. And I believe your room might be the perfect place for me to camp during the winter."

"Hey, that would be swell!" Jimmy exclaimed.

"Now run along and get me that libation," Mr. Pilgrim said.

Jimmy found the green bottle and carefully poured some of the golden liquid into a small glass. But when he turned around, he saw both of his parents standing in the doorway of the den.

"Jimmy, I'm afraid this has gone too far," said his father.

"You mean, you know about me and Mr. Pilgrim?"

"Yes," said Jimmy's mother. "We've secretly watched you from our bedroom window at night, talking out by the mailbox. And Jimmy, we knew something wasn't right because you've become very quiet, and you often cry in your sleep."

"But that's not Mr. Pilgrim's fault!" Jimmy protested. "I just have bad dreams sometimes, because the world is such a cruel place, and all my friends will turn against me someday."

"Don't go back outside," his father said. "We'll handle this, and tomorrow everything will be back to normal."

The next morning, Jimmy watched from inside the house while a police car pulled up to the curb and his parents had a short conversation with two officers. Then one of the policeman opened the mailbox. Jimmy turned away from the window. In a moment his parents came back into the house.

"Why do they have to take him to jail?" Jimmy said. "He's always lived outdoors. He used to hunt with Daniel Boone!"

"Jimmy," said his father, "that man never knew Daniel Boone. He's a 46-year-old drifter named Chester Larkin Freewater, and he has a chemical dependency. Now he'll get the counseling he needs, and a bath. The police did a thorough investigation of his previous arrests."

"But I don't understand," Jimmy said. "If you knew all this from the start, why did you let him stay so long?"

"Evicting a freeloader is tricky," said Jimmy's mother. "First we had to be sure he wasn't, in fact, a magical being."

"And after that," said Jimmy's father, "we had to find out whether or not he had access to a high-powered lawyer. When we established conclusively that he was just a no-account loser who couldn't possibly cause any trouble for us, it was goodbye time."

"I sincerely hope you've learned an important lesson from this," said his mother.

"I sure have," said Jimmy. "Next time I'll ask for at least two forms of identification when somebody tells me they've been alive for hundreds of years. Is that what you mean?"

"Yes, but there's more," said his father. "You see, son, even if a person *has* been alive for centuries, they have no right to talk trash about your parents. And, most important, always remember that you will never, *ever* find true happiness in life by following the ill-conceived advice of a smarmy little whiner who lives in someone else's mailbox."

Going to the Dogs

This is the best year I've had in the hot-dog business. If I were asked to make a sacrifice to help the national economy, I would do it in a minute.
> —Chester Anderson, *Newsweek*, November 1992

We had it all, but now it's gone. Dreams scattered like ashes in the wind. I should have known it couldn't last. Major sectors of the economy dazed and reeling, the steel industry gutted, auto plants closing, timber workers shivering in the dark, but none of us was worried, no sir! We were grilling gold! America's appetite was insatiable!

What did that old Greek philosopher say? Something like "Give me a place to stand and a tube steak long enough and I'll feed the world." I found that magic spot at the corner of Broadway and Jefferson in downtown Portland, Oregon, and thought I would never look back.

I remember when our train came in. It was a few months after the Gulf War ended. The oil fields in Kuwait were still in flames and Saddam was sitting pretty. Our leaders had squandered the fruits of victory, and it made people jittery and uneasy. Where could they turn for reassurance that our traditional values were still being maintained?

My inventory started selling out before noon each day, and I noticed that customers no longer shrugged good-naturedly when I put out the 'Closed' sign. They were anxious. You could almost feel the tension boiling up and down the sidewalks. I called my cousin Ernie in San Francisco, who runs a cart in the financial district, and said, "What's it like where you are?" and he said, "It's crazy! They come at me like animals!"

Sales doubled, tripled, went off the chart. I got my wife's ex-husband to operate a stand for me at the waterfront, and then his parole officer asked if he could get in on the deal, so I set him up after work at the Park 'n' Ride Transit Mall in Beaverton. I realized it was time to start getting organized.

The newsletter was just a front. After the first few issues established our subscriber list, I switched over to phones and faxes for the really important stuff. Sure it sounds paranoid, but I believe success thrives in anonymity. Everyone stopped using their real names once the network was firmly in place.

"No publicity!" was my ongoing mantra. Don't shoot off your mouth. Nothing creates a populist backlash faster than instant wealth. If people want to know how it's going, just nod and then change the subject. Discuss world affairs or Sally Jesse Raphael.

"We're definitely riding the tiger here," read a message from Beef Lips in upstate New York. "I could stay open all night if only my ankles would stop swelling. Lord, it hurts so good."

Rat Hair in Los Angeles was even more eloquent. "I believe we have a rendezvous with destiny," he wrote in. "Too bad Will and Ariel Durant aren't around to see this."

We couldn't keep the lid on completely, of course. I thought the game was up when *A Current Affair* started zeroing in on those crazy girls down in Florida, you know, the ones who wore string bikinis and parked their carts beside busy highways. Luckily we had a contact in the area, Bone Chip; he convinced those gals to cut back on their hours, and things settled down again.

Heaven knows I tried to practice what I preached. Kept the old Datsun running, stayed away from nightclubs, and dumped all the profits into no-load mutual funds. Gold chains never latched around my extremities.

Yeah, we all promised ourselves we wouldn't get cocky, but when you're swimming in a river of money, you can't imagine the headwaters will ever go dry.

I saw a fax one day from Beef Lips that said he was thinking of making a bid on the Empire State Building. Then Rat Hair mentioned in a phone conversation that he wanted to buy the Queen Mary and move it from Long Beach to a theme park called Gristle Town he was going to build out near Indio.

I was planning a generous endowment to the Home Economics department at Oregon State for a new Meat By-Products Research Lab. After that, maybe a movie deal, something with Cindy Crawford.

And then, without warning, all hell broke loose. One smart remark uttered on a street corner in New Orleans and the pollsters and pundits were on us like wolves. Suddenly everybody's demanding to know why the hot dog business is so darn wonderful when the rest of the USA is hung out to dry.

Before I could swallow hard, the IRS had two agents stationed beside me on the sidewalk scribbling in little notebooks every time I scratched my head, and videotaping each person who so much as grabbed a paper napkin to blow his or her nose.

Then came the personalized letter from the President. "Thank you!" it began. "Your willingness to make a sacrifice to help the national economy is most appreciated." I called Ernie in San Francisco, but his phone was disconnected.

Pushcarts began to proliferate in the downtown area and their prices were cutthroat. I checked with my wholesaler to find out what was happening, and he said the entire region was being swamped with cheap wieners from overseas. "They're trying to balance the trade deficit on our backs," he said. "I just got a letter from the President explaining the whole thing."

The fatal mistake was not covering our behinds in Washington. I called my congressman to talk about the possibility of protective legislation, but all I got was a lecture on open markets and my role in the new global village.

Talk about irony! I used to laugh when customers told me they worried about insect parts and clothing fibers in our food supply. Do you know what they use for filler in Southeast Asia? Chicken beaks and old tires, mostly. I found that out one day when I sold one of those cheap imports to the mayor, who took a large bite and promptly broke one of her teeth on a valve stem.

The lawsuits and the high insurance rates and the public antagonism were more than I could handle. Without Chapter 11, I'd probably be living in the hills outside Eugene right now, trying to survive on pine nuts and boiled moss. I can't even think about frankfurters now without getting a knot in my stomach. And don't think the situation is going to improve anytime soon.

You probably heard about that freighter incident out here, the North Korean ship that caught fire. The owners said it was carrying patio furniture, but I know for a fact the cargo hold was chock full of landfill-quality hot links headed for the Northwest market. The news people also failed to mention anything about how the smoke clouds from that giant weenie roast drifted in over Coos Bay and blistered the paint on every car parked along the waterfront.

Morning in America? Excuse me if I skip breakfast.

The Last Best Hope

Do you want to spend your next vacation scavenging for scraps at the dump instead of relaxing on the beach at Cancun? Many happy returns. Do you enjoy watching your children eat clay for dinner when they could be feasting on steak and lobster? Hey, you're the chef.

Now that I've got your attention, maybe you'll listen to reason. I'm talking about money, investments, financial security, and all those other great ideas that show up on the nightly news but never in your back pocket, if you get my drift.

My name is Ed. I can't tell you my last name because it would cause panic among the big boys, the ones who control *everything*. I used to work for them, but now I share their secrets with my subscribers, and that could be you, chum.

THIS IS NOT JUNK MAIL. I got your name and address from a special limited-access polling list called 'People Who Would Save Themselves If They Only Knew How.' Say Amen!

Did you know this letter has gone around the world at least ten times? Well it has, and that's because the language of $$$$ is universal.

In Argentina, General Gumbo ignored my advice to jump on MightyBank (NYSE: MTB) at $12 per share and three days later he was court-martialed and sent to prison. Luckily his wife found the letter, followed my instructions, and now lives comfortably in a nice duplex in upstate New York.

People ask me, "Why should I believe this?"

Look, if you were standing in the crosswalk of a busy intersection and suddenly felt like you were about to vomit, wouldn't it be nice if someone ran up and handed you an airsick bag? Well, that's my point.

You *can* have it all. There's plenty to go around, and I explain how to get it each month in *Ed's Report*. I've named my strategy 'The Secret of UNSTOPPABLE WEALTH.' If you pick up the phone and call right now, the first issue will be in your mailbox in less time than it takes to construct an elaborate fantasy world of endless material gratification and physical pleasure. Have your ZIP Code ready!

With that first issue you'll learn the Ten Shocking Facts About Stockbrokers, plus my favorite self-defense tips to help you disarm and subdue muggers, stickup men, and international bankers.

Here's a recent testimonial:

Dear Ed—After years of living in a culvert I read an old copy of your newsletter. By following your strategy I was able to retire later in the afternoon that same day. I now own several estates and consider myself almost a living god.

> Sincerely,
> Angus M.
> Cutlery, AZ

Unfortunately, Angus died two weeks after this letter was written when he was accidentally crushed by a huge canvas bag stuffed with U.S. currency that was carelessly thrown from an armored car as it was being unloaded onto his patio, where he had fallen asleep reading *The Wall Street Journal*. So don't get complacent.

And don't be fooled by my competitors who promise to give you "inside information" on the market. I learned a long time ago that if you think you're going to outsmart everybody by eavesdropping on whispered conversations in public restrooms, the first thing you discover when you step outside is that your pants are missing. Trust me on this.

If you call now and subscribe for two years, you will also receive a ground-to-air signaling beacon and my personal handbook of non-alternative energy sources.

Remember that in the $$$$ game a good defense is crucial for protecting your gains, but when most people think about defense the only ones that come to mind are (1) zone, (2) man-to-man, or (3) Nimzo-Indian. I'M NOT LYING!

What's that? You believe the market is just going to keep getting better and you don't need my advice? Well, I know people who believe that all the fliers of the 'Lost Patrol' who vanished in 1947 off the Florida coast are actually living in a dormitory at Cape Canaveral, and they've all tested HIV positive. Which makes it kind of a toss-up, wouldn't you say?

If you call now and order a gift subscription for a friend, you will receive all the premiums mentioned *plus* the secret NASA satellite photos of the Martian cities *and* a special first-edition *Cookbook for the Coming Hard Times*, which features many award-winning recipes including my famous 'Mock Abalone Delight' (the secret's in the tuna).

Do you know the three worst mistakes every beginning investor makes? Two of them involve your own body parts, but I won't say any more because we're starting to waste time. There may be a globalist moving into your neighborhood right now.

Here's another testimonial:

I will give up my subscription to your publication when they pry it from my cold, dead hands.

Sheena K.
Cornerstone, NV

Don't wait one more nanosecond. Knowing how to take your own pulse won't do any good if your heart has already stopped! No guts, no glory! CAN YOU PROVE IT ISN'T TRUE?

The Battle for HyperMart

When the chairman, Mr. Collingwood, first told me of the mission, I could not have been more appalled.

"This is bloody-well top secret," he said. "Management of the HyperMart has reneged on its acceptance of our buy-out offer. We have signed agreements and paid earnest money, and the firm needs that store desperately if we are to improve our sales figures. Since the blighters are trying to back out, we have no choice but to take it by force. *You* will lead the assault."

As a lad, I had always delighted in our family outings at the HyperMart, with long lazy days of leisurely wandering through the hundreds of departments. It is still hard to believe that a single store can sprawl across hundreds of acres and contain every possible item for household use. Now it seemed I would browse through this ultimate development in one-stop shopping under much more difficult circumstances.

It was decided that a daylight operation would offer the best chance of total surprise and thereby maximize the odds in our favor. We also felt that a joint Anglo-American effort, using divisions from our U.S. subsidiaries, would discourage interference from competitors who might have their own take-over plans.

I admit that I was not terribly confident as we neared H-hour. The troops in my landing craft were mostly support personnel yanked from headquarters at the last minute. A few had some background in merchandising, but most had never set foot in the kind of vast 'post-mall' environment we would be faced with.

Fortunately there wasn't time to dwell on these short-comings. With clockwork efficiency, our boats ran ashore at the Picnic Lagoon precisely at oh-11-hundred hours, and there was virtually no opposition as the men stormed up the grassy slopes to the Snack Bar. I had serious uncertainties about how the staff would react, but after some brief negotiations and the promise of an extra week of vacation in their next contract, all the food handlers defected to our side without hesitation.

My men passed out candy and cigarettes, and in return the workers handed over the keys to the employee washrooms. I quickly dispatched a scout team to begin sealing off those cubicles for our own use.

While the amphibious operations were proceeding smartly, some of the other phases of the assault were experiencing complications. Colonel Hawkins Weatherbee had planned to lead his 101st Airborne Overnight Delivery Brigade in a 'coup de main' onto the roof of the administration building, but unexpected gusty winds carried most of their gliders into a remote area of the south parking lot.

Luckily, Weatherbee was able to commandeer a number of jitneys and shuttle his men to the main entrance, where they secured several moving walkways and made ready to advance into the covered promenade.

Farther to the west, Brigadier Digby Hammond-Hammond was having problems of a different kind. His main force had seized the loading dock behind Fresh Produce and was supposed to launch a two-pronged attack toward Cold Cuts and Frozen Foods.

But unknown to Hammond-Hammond, store clerks had switched the aisle markers in anticipation of a possible attack. Sergeant Andrew Ebersol, in command of the lead platoon, had advanced several hundred yards when he realized something was wrong. Before he could turn his men back, they were hopelessly tangled up in Oriental Foods and Spices, far from the original objective.

Ebersol showed great initiative in abandoning the original plan and, instead, moving directly upon the checkout counters. The cashiers, seeing their situation was hopeless, chose to flee rather than surrender. This could have caused serious trouble, as the checkout lines were already long, and a disorganized mob of angry patrons could have disrupted the movement of our units.

But Ebersol immediately directed a small force of his men to take over the registers. "Most of those boys had never made change before," he said later, "but this is a 'can-do' outfit if I ever saw one."

Meanwhile, disaster was looming at Garden Supplies. Major Peabody Prestwick had established his command post amongst a display of lawn furniture and was preparing to make contact with the lead units of the 101st, which had been moving steadily south since taking control of the promenade.

The plan called for a link-up at Sundries, and then the combined force would wheel and drive eastward down Aisle 17 through Sporting Goods and Office Needs, rolling up any opposition along the way.

But just as Prestwick was preparing to advance, forward observers radioed back that a large force was moving in from the direction of Auto Accessories. We learned later that some of the more fanatical supply clerks had changed into civilian dress and were trying to incite the customers into open resistance by spreading ugly rumors of blanket price increases. If our perimeter line had been broken by the approaching force, it would have jeopardized the main thrust of the operation.

Into this pivotal moment stepped Captain Eddie Steinberg, one of the American liaison officers attached to Prestwick's command. "In one of the most brilliant field improvisations I have ever witnessed," Prestwick wrote in his after-action report, "Captain Steinberg raced alone into Bathroom Luxuries, captured a squad of courtesy clerks, and then grabbed a public address phone to announce a 'Blue Light Special' on shower curtains and Calgon Body Moisturizer. This diverted the approaching force away from our positions and completely broke the opposition's hopes for a counter-offensive."

Such calm feats of heroism were not uncommon. The 4th Duke of Cornwall's Jiffy-Lube Volunteers were supposed to attack up the central escalator and secure Tools and Hardware. Instead, an outdated map led them smack into the middle of Lingerie, much to the consternation of their leader, Lt. Morrisrow Hanley.

"These men had been draining engine blocks at our oil-changing subsidiary only hours earlier," he said. "Many still had grease under their fingernails, yet there they were, surrounded by filmy undergarments and satiny stockings. To their credit, not one man broke from the line, and we were able to make a lateral swing into Fine Furniture without losing momentum."

In the end, the long push down Aisle 17 succeeded in cutting all remaining lines of communication between Administration and the main floor. We confronted the manager, a terribly truculent fellow named Bukovski, in his office, and he absolutely refused to speak with us until I informed him of our employee profit-sharing plan. After that he caved in, and it was just a matter of mopping up.

As in any battle, we came upon some vile discoveries afterward. Inventory control had been abandoned for some time, and many storage areas were jammed with rotting, outdated merchandise. One crate contained seven hundred Mr. Ed school lunchboxes. Workers we de-briefed also said that bait-and-switch schemes were rampant and that entire departments had been on the verge of complete anarchy.

Now the HyperMart is a friendly, peaceful environment. Seeing the long rows of splendid displays on a recent anniversary visit, it was hard for me to imagine what a strange turn history might have taken had we failed in our mission.

I walked to the Bathroom Luxuries counter, where Captain Steinberg had made his propitious announcement over the public address system. A bright-eyed young clerk approached me.

"Can I help you?" she said. "We're having a red tag sale on shower curtains and Calgon Body Moisturizer."

"Are you now?" I said. It was clear she had no idea who I was or why those particular items are placed on sale at this time every year. Slowly, the sharp edges of the past are blunted. But we who were there will always remember.

"Yes," I said, "I shall have a look-see at the shower curtains." She led me to the sale table, past happy families shopping with confidence, valued customers who were getting honest quality at reasonable prices, and I thought of the old saying: There is no substitute for victory.

Safe House

"Wake up! Wake up!"

My eyes snapped open, and in the dim light I was confronted by the stricken, ravaged face of Florence Henderson.

"I have a headache THIS BIG!" she said frantically, stretching out her arms in both directions.

"Calm down," I said. "This is where you need to be."

Her hands were ice cold and trembling as I led her down the stairs. We sat at the kitchen table while she sipped a glass of orange juice.

"Tastes just like fresh-squeezed," she said, choking back tears. "Look, I'm sorry to barge in like this, but I didn't know where else to turn. Something's terribly wrong, and nobody will listen!"

"I know what you're going through," I said. "For years you touted the benefits of chicken fried in bubbling hot vegetable oil. Now you're seized by doubts about the true meaning of those statements, and your head is spinning with the echoes of other promotional claims."

"My God!" she said. "That's what I've been trying to tell people!" She raised the glass to her lips and drained it with a determined expression. "Good to the last drop," she said, and then her shoulders sagged as she began to sob disconsolately.

At that moment, heavy footsteps thudded down the hall. We both looked toward the kitchen doorway as the rugged, imposing figure of Brigadier General Chuck Yeager (Ret.) loomed into view. His yellow flight suit seemed radiant, and the lightning bolts on his helmet gleamed with a fresh coat of lacquer as he strode into the room.

"Do you want to see something?" he said, slamming his fists onto the table. "My skin is so chapped that I can write the word 'dry' on the back of my own hand!" As we watched in awed silence, he carefully scratched out the large block letters with a fingernail. Then he did it again on the back of *my* hand.

"If I don't look good, you don't look good!" he cautioned. Florence opened her mouth to speak, but the feisty living legend of American aviation was out the door in two quick strides.

"What in tarnation is wrong with *him*?" she asked. "I knew he didn't have any manners, but I thought he only worried about spark plugs."

"He's confused and upset, just as you are," I said calmly, and there was a glimmer of recognition in her expression.

"You mean—?"

"That's right, Flo. You're not alone. It's a malady that strikes many celebrities without warning. The clinical term is Post-Endorsement Trauma Syndrome. PETS, if you prefer.

"It's characterized by a sudden inability to differentiate between major commercial campaigns, along with other symptoms such as loss of self-respect and periods of uncontrollable rage."

"How do you spell relief?" she said. "Can anything be done?"

I reached out and took her hands in mine. "It's tough," I said. "You just have to learn how to take a licking and keep on ticking."

My mind drifted back to the first time I encountered this fearful condition that threatens anyone who speaks out on behalf of brand-name merchandise. I was out for a drive one day when I swerved to avoid hitting an elderly man who was sprawled at the edge of the road. I stopped the car and went over to see if he needed help. His clothes were torn and dirty, and I assumed he was a local derelict.

"You okay, mister?" I asked, pulling him up to a sitting position. His eyes were glazed with pain, and in a raspy voice he whispered, "The quality goes in before the name goes on." It was Euell Gibbons.

This pioneer of the natural foods movement had been reduced to a quivering shell of a human, so I took him back to my house for a hot shower and a square meal.

"How do you feel now?" I asked innocently.

"Finger lickin' good," he smiled, and that's when I knew something was seriously wrong.

During the next few weeks he poured out the bitter details of his life as a paid spokesperson. It was an endless charade of breakfast speeches in backwater towns, autograph sessions at bookstores in perimeter malls, and the constant pressure to perform on cue when the TV cameras started rolling.

"And what good is all the money if you're too tired and bewildered to spend it?" he said. "When I looked at where my life was heading, I finally said, 'Hey, it's not how long you make it. It's how you make it long.' But I guess it was too late by then. Next thing I remember is lyin' out there where you found me."

I've heard the same feelings of disillusionment repeated over and over by a legion of famous voices. Don't ask me how anyone discovers this place. I've never sought any publicity.

But after Euell left, the news got around. My phone number seems to be known in all the right places, traveling by word of mouth in hushed tones. They all find out where I am, and sooner or later they end up here.

"Come on," I told Florence. "I want to show you around."

"Will I be here very long?"

"That all depends on you," I said. "Everyone is different, and they recover at their own pace. Look in here for a second."

I opened the door to a small room that was unfurnished except for a single barstool. A tall, athletic man was seated on it in a pose reminiscent of a Rodin sculpture.

"My stars!" she gasped. "It's Jim Palmer! And he's stark naked!"

"He's totally forgotten how to dress himself," I said. "Came in here three days ago, ripped his underwear to shreds, and just sits there." At that moment the former major league all-star looked over at us with a forlorn expression.

"This I do for me," he said quietly, and I closed the door.

"The key thing," I said, "is to stay isolated from all forms of mass media. Exposure to any kind of promotional announcement will only aggravate the persistent anxiety."

Just then I felt a sudden blow to my head, and I realized we were being attacked. Florence was knocked over backward, but showed her true spirit by fighting back gamely.

Our assailants were both young women. They were not very powerful and seemed more interested in battling with each other. In a few moments we had them pinned against a wall.

"We don't bite, we don't even light!" they screamed in unison.

"I've never felt such overwhelming hostility," Florence hissed at me. "Who are they?"

"The Doublemint Twins," I said. "Years of carefully acting out every bodily movement in tandem has caused them to develop intense feelings of self-loathing, which they transfer onto each other and onto anyone who happens to be close by. They were supposed to be tranquilized, but it's obvious I'll have to increase the dose."

Florence helped me get the Twins sedated and securely anchored in the sensory-deprivation pool.

One of the girls looked up at us dreamily and said, "Can anyone make a detergent that softens your hands while you do the dishes?"

"You're soaking in it," I said, zipping the hood closed on her rubber body suit.

Florence was trembling again by the time we got back to the kitchen, and I noticed she was beginning to perspire.

"I guess I'm just overwhelmed by it all," she said. "Am I really going to get better?"

"You'll recover," I said, "and you'll endorse again."

"I'm so grateful," she said, "that someone like you still exists, someone who is willing to take on such a grueling, thankless job for the benefit of others. Why do you do it, year after year?"

I gazed deeply into her eyes and felt her spirit reaching out to me with hope and trust. What special secrets would I learn about this gifted woman who galvanized millions of TV viewers during five unforgettable seasons on *The Brady Bunch*?

I stepped close to her. Our lips were just inches apart, and I knew that in a matter of seconds we would be locked in a passionate embrace.

"Florence," I said, "there's one thing you have to keep in mind. This isn't just a job. It's an adventure."

And Justice For All

"I'm not sure this case had any winners," said the burly, bearded prosecutor, his voice tight with emotion, "but it's a case that demanded vigorous action from our legal system, and I'm satisfied with the outcome. I hope the victims will feel a sense of closure and find a way to move on with their lives."

With that, Santa Clara County Deputy District Attorney Lancelot Harrington III finished reading the text of his surprising official statement, stepped back from the array of microphones, and wiped his sweating forehead with a handkerchief as the press room erupted in a roar of shouted questions from reporters.

Harrington's sudden and unexpected announcement of a plea bargain agreement came on the eve of what many legal experts had predicted would be one of the most contentious and controversial courtroom battles since the Scopes 'monkey' trial of 1923. The settlement means the American public will be spared from having to endure a gaudy and grotesque media event. But the furious debate this case has raised among child protective agencies, civil libertarians, animal rights advocates, and literary scholars will not be fading away any time soon.

Had the case proceeded, it would have gone into the law books as 'State of California v. Wellington Brittany Precious Perfection of Zamboni.' The defendant's legal name reflected his distinguished feline lineage. To the general public, however, he will always be known simply as The Cat in the Hat.

20813670

20813670

"He comes from a prestigious family of Cornish Rex show champions," said Harrington during a recent interview on Court TV. "He could have been a role model, but something went wrong."

The 'something' he referred to was an incident that occurred in the mid-1950s, on a day when 'the sun did not shine' and 'it was too wet to play.' Investigators say the exact date may never be known. What *is* beyond dispute is that the Cat, without being provoked or enticed, entered a private residence on a quiet street in Sunnyvale, California, and proceeded to interact with two young children who had been left alone temporarily.

A fictionalized version of the encounter was later released in book form and enjoyed great popularity among youthful readers. No one involved in its publication appeared to have any knowledge that the story was reality-based.

The deception ended, as often happens, by sheer coincidence. While vacationing in Mexico last year, Deputy D.A. Harrington stopped briefly at a small roadside aquatic park. As he strolled among large, murky tanks of foul-smelling water, he heard a splash, and a voice called to him in English.

In a sworn statement, Harrington described his astonishing conversation with an elderly, malnourished aquarium-dweller who claimed to have been the victim of a terrifying home invasion many years earlier. The informant, who did not want his name revealed for fear of possible reprisals, was identified in court papers only as 'The Fish.'

"How he ended up in Mexico, I don't know," Harrington said later. "But he lived with this awful secret for most of his life, wrestling with inner shame and guilt. Remember, in the book version the Fish was the only character who clearly understood that the Cat was out of control.

However, during the incident, he was confined to a glass bowl and then a teapot, and thus could not do anything to stop the action. It's incredible that he finally hooked up with an official who has legal jurisdiction in the area where the crime took place."

Physically and emotionally drained by the long ordeal, the Fish expired a few days after the chance meeting, but by then he had given Harrington a veritable shopping list of names, locations, and other previously unknown details. Armed with this information, the D.A.'s office and the county Children's Services Division immediately launched a wide-ranging investigation.

Indictments were quickly handed down by a grand jury, and an arrest warrant was issued for the Cat. He was soon discovered living with a retired couple in a drab residential hotel just a few miles up the Peninsula in Redwood City.

In a bizarre twist, the Cat initially denied any wrong-doing, but then offered to lead investigators to the home of the two victims, with whom he had remained in regular contact during the intervening years.

Despite intense press coverage, the real names of the two siblings never leaked out to any news organization. Mental health experts who interviewed the pair described them as being in a constant state of fear, anxiety, and depression, and insisted that they be shielded from the media. Officially they were known as 'John Doe' and 'Sister Sally.'

The peculiar nature of the incident and its close connection to a famous children's book aroused immediate public attention. The atmosphere became even more highly charged when superstar defense lawyer Robert Shapiro called a press conference to announce that he was offering his services to the Cat *pro bono*, an offer that was instantly accepted and all but guaranteed daily television coverage of each new development in the proceedings.

One of the first and most serious obstacles facing the prosecution was a reluctance on the part of the victims to confirm any criminal behavior by the Cat. "It was obvious they were still intimidated by him," Harrington said. "His benign appearance conceals a calculating, sinister personality."

The prosecution responded with the controversial strategy of subjecting both victims to extensive interviews under hypnosis in an effort to find recovered memories of the encounter. They claimed the effort was unusually successful.

"In separate evaluations," Harrington reported afterward, "they told substantially the same story. I won't give details except to say there was trauma. There was pain. This was not the fun and games portrayed in the book. An innocent boy and girl were emotionally violated. John Doe suffers from chronic migraine headaches. Sally never finished high school. They've been unable to move away from that house or develop any kind of normal relationship with the rest of society."

Defense attorney Shapiro didn't waste any time in criticizing the prosecution for failing to come up with corroborating testimony to support the allegations of abuse. He also attempted to shift responsibility for the encounter away from the Cat.

"Where was the mother during this episode?" he demanded during one of the preliminary hearings. "Why were two young children left alone on this 'cold, cold wet day'? My client, I'm confident to say, would never have entered the house if an adult had been present. The mother, by her absence, helped cause the interaction that took place. She was the enabler."

There was no testimony from either parent, since both had passed away many years earlier. Without any direct rebuttal, some legal observers felt Shapiro's tactics might succeed in making his client appear to be a co-victim in the case.

But even as the defense seemed to be building a solid foundation, prosecutors were doggedly pursuing valuable leads. The major break came when they located Julius and Jonathan Himmelsbach, twin brothers who had achieved marginal success on the midget wrestling circuit as The Doomsday Duo. When questioned, both men admitted having been accomplices of the Cat during their troubled teenage years. The relationship apparently had vague spiritual overtones. The twins claimed the Cat told them to discard their personal histories and began addressing them only as 'Thing One' and 'Thing Two.'

"It was insidious," said one investigator. "Those boys were extremely vulnerable. They had blue hair. They were physiologically ambiguous. And the Cat exploited their emotional insecurity for his own purposes. He's a master manipulator."

With evidence against his client mounting, Robert Shapiro shifted gears, dropping all criticism of the victim's parents and expanding the defense team to include Leslie Abramson, a respected veteran of the Menendez Brothers trial. Together they devised a new strategy. The most controversial aspect of the plan was its reliance on testimony obtained from the Cat during several episodes of 'past life regression.'

After their first request for a hearing on the subject was rejected, Shapiro and Abramson appealed to public opinion. Several celebrities, including Dionne Warwick and Shirley MacLaine, signed an open letter to the judge urging him to reconsider his position on eternal life. At no time was there a hint that plea bargain talks were underway.

While the announcement of the plea agreement came as a surprise, the terms were not extraordinary. Charges were reduced to two counts of felony child endangerment and one count of misdemeanor trespassing. In return for a guilty plea, the Cat was sentenced to ten years of supervised probation and ordered to cease all contact with the victims. None of the principals were willing to speak with reporters, and all three were spirited out of the courthouse at the very moment that Deputy D.A. Harrington was officially announcing the details of the settlement.

Perhaps realizing that the sudden conclusion of the case would come under intense and perhaps harsh media scrutiny, the defense and prosecution teams took the unusual step of standing side by side on the podium at the news conference, as if huddling together for solidarity against the expected verbal barrage.

While both sides agreed that the negotiated ending was preferable to a long, expensive trial that might have caused additional psychological damage to some of the participants, there was no backing down from their established positions.

The defense team insisted that their 'past life regression' gambit was viable and would have been effective in swaying a jury. "What we have determined," said Shapiro, "is that in a previous existence the defendant was a mouse. As such, he was tormented constantly by cats. In his present life, he was simply reacting to those past events by becoming the tormenter."

Abramson pointed out that tests conducted by the defense proved the Cat also displayed symptoms of attention deficit hyperactivity disorder. "That's why he spoke in rhymes," she said. "It was the only way he could remember what he was doing."

Prosecutor Harrington disagreed emphatically. "The rhyming was just his way of ritualizing the abuse," he countered. "It wasn't overtly satanic, but he was headed down that road."

By the end of the news conference, all the attorneys were visibly tired and hoarse. As reporters left to file their stories, someone asked Harrington if the case had changed him.

"They all do," he said, almost in a whisper. "Little by little, I lose more of my illusions. I used to think happy endings only occurred in kid's stories. But now, quite obviously, even that isn't true anymore."

Media Glare Misses
A Cage Classic

While sports reporters all over the country were once again transfixed by the NCAA basketball frenzy known as March Madness, no coverage at all was given to the equally exciting NA3U (National Association of Unusual and Unpublicized Universities) playoffs and the inspiring victory of little Edgar Cayce Institute in the championship game.

This season's finale was held at the Cayce campus in upstate New York, within the dank confines of the old brick fieldhouse that students affectionately call Spookville. The nickname is a sly reference to Cayce's distinction of being the only American university that offers a curriculum entirely devoted to the study of paranormal phenomena.

The Golden Enigmas were led by 6'10" center Pekka Kalkonnen, a transfer student from Helsinki who earned Player of the Year honors in the Big Strange Conference despite the fact that he had never touched a basketball prior to enrolling last fall.

But Kalkonnen's burly physique and eerie powers of premonition resulted in 127 blocked shots and 98 steals during the regular season (both school records), and opposing players quickly dubbed him The Human Ouija Board.

The championship game found the O-man and his team pitted against an upstart squad from Police State of Lima, Ohio. The Thin Blue Line, making its first appearance in the finals, had blown past all its rivals in the Mid-Eccentric Association and then survived a wild semifinal contest against Central Petroleum.

The C-P Demon Drillers, surprise champs of the always-strong Peculiar Eight, actually led State by 19 points at halftime in the semis and seemed firmly in control. But Blue Line Coach Winston 'Sarge' Tubbs engineered a sudden turnaround by having all five Central Petroleum starters picked up during intermission and held for questioning until the last four minutes of the game. Final score: Blue Line 122, Drillers 105.

Since Police State and Cayce had no common opponents, it was difficult to predict how the teams would match up. But the Enigmas became sentimental favorites after school officials announced that 85-year-old Thaddeus Kleinfelter, who had served a dual role as president and head basketball coach since the college was founded, would be retiring at the end of the current academic year.

The stress of holding both jobs had begun to adversely affect Kleinfelter's coaching abilities, as evidenced by several bouts of memory loss and sudden personality changes. One of the oddest incidents occurred near the end of Cayce's 96-70 drubbing of Survivalist College in the opening round of the tournament.

With less than a minute remaining in the game, Kleinfelter called a timeout for no apparent reason. Then, instead of setting up a play, he lapsed into a trance and began speaking in a German-accented voice that called itself Helmut and told several risqué stories about life as a gay blacksmith in fourteenth-century Dresden. Later, he disclaimed any recollection of the speech.

The championship contest featured rough play by both teams in the first half. State tried to rattle Kalkonnen by talking trash and calling him 'Sorenninkkivalltukbillip,' a Finnish epithet that means 'one who eats hoofs of the reindeer.' But the big man was unfazed, and the Enigmas led 45-36 at the half.

State also missed a golden opportunity to mount a comeback midway through the second half, when the referees noticed a mysterious figure drifting in the air near midcourt. They promptly whistled Cayce for using an illegal six-man offense.

(Game films later showed the apparition was dressed in a Civil War uniform and bore a strong resemblance to the notorious confederate raider John Singleton Mosby. "He looked familiar," quipped Kalkonnen, who is majoring in American history. "If he hadn't been incorporeal, I would have thrown him a lob pass.")

Despite protests from Cayce, State was awarded two technical foul shots and possession of the ball, but it wasn't enough. The Blue Line players seemed visibly shaken by their spectral encounter, and three of them refused to cross the 10-second stripe during the final six minutes.

As the clock ran down, Kalkonnen ran wild, scoring 23 of his game-high 47 points and even displaying hints of telekinetic powers by altering the path of two three-point shots after the ball had left his hands. Looking up at the final score of 89-67, Sarge Tubbs could only shrug and recite the Police State school motto: "There oughta be a law," he sighed.

The postgame news conference was brief and, as in past years, sparsely attended. The only media representatives on hand were a field producer for *Unsolved Mysteries*, a research assistant from *Fate* magazine, two stringers for the *Weekly*

World News, a camera operator from the local cable access channel, and Whitley Strieber.

After the ceremonial presentation of the championship trophy, Thaddeus Kleinfelter was asked if he was sorry to be stepping down. Leaning toward the microphone to answer, Coach 'K' suddenly stiffened and then fell forward onto the podium. After groaning incoherently for several minutes, he abruptly straightened up and, with smoke pouring out of both ears, bellowed, *"I am the god of hell fire!!"*

In the absence of any further questions, the gathering was quickly adjourned and the onlookers fled.

New Leash on Life

Driving along the narrow, tree-lined road toward the kennel, I noticed the first blossoms of spring in the branches that hung out over the pavement. The scenic beauty of the place had always impressed me. And my golden retriever, Bigfoot, had come to think of it as his second home.

I parked the car, walked into the waiting area, and pushed the 'call' button. Usually the harsh sound of the buzzer would set off a chorus of yelps and howls from the pens in the back yard. But now, everything was strangely quiet. The absence of noise made me uneasy. I had an immediate premonition that something out of the ordinary was going to happen on this visit.

Hastings, the owner/manager, opened the door and stepped into the room. He was wearing a white lab coat, as usual, which gave him a scientific bearing. This image was enhanced by a head of disheveled gray hair and a drooping moustache. He looked like a younger cousin of Albert Einstein. Hastings was leading Bigfoot on a simple nylon rope, which he handed to me.

"If you would, please," he said, "take him to the car and come back to my office. I'd like a few words with you."

My faithful companion seemed forlorn as I led him outside. He jumped into the back seat of the car without enthusiasm, and then sat quietly as I slipped the cord from around his neck.

The kennel office had a separate entrance around the side of the building. It was a spacious room, dominated by a massive oak desk that would have been more appropriately situated in the executive suite of a conservative British bank president.

Hastings was seated behind the desk. The lab coat had been removed, and I saw that he was attired in a navy blue cardigan and gray slacks. His eyes were clear and alert, and as I sat down in front of the desk he sighed deeply.

"As you know, Mr. Jensen," he began, "things haven't been the same around this place since my wife died last year. Dorthea was the real brains of the whole operation. She had high blood pressure, as I've probably told you."

"You did mention it once," I said. Hastings' wife had suffered a fatal stroke one afternoon while attempting to lift a 50-pound bag of kibble shortly before feeding time.

"Well, I just can't keep the place going without her," Hastings said. "I've been closing down slowly, so that I could speak with all our loyal clients and thank them personally for supporting us. Today, in fact, is the end. I wanted you to be the very last customer. I hope you understand my situation."

"I do, and I can't say I'm surprised," I said. "You've had a hard time. I appreciate how you've cared for my dog. He loves this place. Do you have any suggestions for a new place? I'll be needing to board him again next week."

"You're a busy man," Hastings said. "Lots of travel. What is your business? Sales?"

"I'm the regional quality control supervisor for a chain of gourmet pastry shops," I explained. "It keeps me on the go."

"Is your outfit the one that brags about the fancy ingredients in each roll?" he asked.

"Yes," I said. "The vanilla comes from Madagascar."

"Goodness," he replied. "I hope the harvesting doesn't threaten any wildlife."

"I . . . don't know anything about that part," I said, hoping he wouldn't pursue the matter, since I had never given the vanilla harvest or its environmental consequences a second thought.

"Here is a list of kennels I can recommend," he said, handing me a piece of paper. "But you may not have any need for them after you hear what I am about to tell you."

With that, Hastings stood up and walked over to another door, which he opened to reveal a small closet. He rummaged among the garments hanging inside and pulled out a beautifully woven, rust-colored blazer. It shimmered with a kind of radiance as he walked over to me.

"This," said Hastings, "is an exact replica of the jacket that is awarded each year to the winner of the Masters Golf Tournament in Augusta. My wife was an avid weaver, and a golf fan as well. She made this especially for you."

"Why is it such an unusual color?" I asked. "Isn't the winner's jacket at the Masters supposed to be green?"

"Because it is made out of your dog's hair," Hastings explained. "Dorthea used to brush him for hours and then spin the fibers into yarn. She was nearly finished when she died. I ended up sewing on the buttons myself. Try it on?"

To my complete surprise, the jacket fit perfectly. "How did you get my measurements?" I asked.

"Dorthea had an incredible knack for judging the nuances of the male torso," Hastings said. "Now, be careful about getting that wet. Personally, I think it smells great in the rain. But some people might think it a bit too musky."

He returned to his seat behind the desk.

"You should include payment for this gift in my final bill," I said, but he quickly shook his head.

"I am not even going to charge you for this last visit," he said. "You may not be fully aware of this, but your dog is a truly unique creature. He and Dorthea had an amazing relationship. Amazing. You aren't married, are you?"

"Er, no," I said. "Bigfoot and I keep bachelors' hall together, so to speak."

"Well, you should know that he enjoys the company of women very much," Hastings said. "Very much, indeed."

"He's always been real cheery after a stay here," I said. "I assumed it was because you gave him special attention, took him on long walks and such."

"Oh, we haven't walked him in years," Hastings said. "I believe, deep down, he intensely dislikes exercise."

"Really? But I've been paying three dollars per day extra for those walks. It's listed right on the receipts."

"I know, I know," said Hastings, "but we weren't trying to cheat you. As a substitute for the walks, we began reading to your dog. And I must tell you, quite honestly, that he's got a marvelous appreciation for the spoken word."

"That doesn't sound like my dog at all," I said. "Bigfoot usually doesn't pay any attention to what I'm saying, unless I've got food in my hand."

"Ah, there's the rub," said Hastings. "Try speaking to him from a more introspective point of view. Don't just issue commands. He's most receptive to narrative fiction that involves some type of human suffering. For example, he was genuinely moved when we finished *The Story of O* by Pauline Reage.

"Why have you waited so long to tell me this?" I asked.

"Different reasons, I guess. We didn't know how you'd react. And part of it was pure selfishness, I admit. We had never encountered a canine with such complex emotional needs, and we certainly didn't want anything to jeopardize our chances to spend time together and develop mutual interests."

"What other interests did you discover?"

"Costume design," he said without hesitation. "Drama, music, performing arts. We compiled a photo album. Come around here and I'll show you."

I looked over Hastings' shoulder as he flipped the pages of a large three-ring binder that contained a number of studio-quality portraits featuring my dog in various guises.

"This is one of my favorites," said Hastings, pointing at what I assumed was some sort of mock wedding scene.

"It's a re-enactment of the coronation of Queen Victoria," he said. "Dorthea is the monarch, and your dog is Prince Albert. I'm a real history nut, in case you hadn't guessed by now."

"And you say Bigfoot enjoyed this?"

"He relished it," Hastings assured me. "Look here, this is wonderful." It was a picture of the dog wearing some kind of Nazi combat uniform. "He's portraying the daring German commando Otto Skorzeny during the rescue of Mussolini."

A few pages later I noticed a picture of Bigfoot, Hastings, and Dorthea all standing next to a life-sized cardboard figure of Elvis Presley.

"That was a spur-of-the-moment thing," Hastings said. "It happened at a souvenir shop near Graceland."

"You took my dog to Memphis?" I said, amazed. "That's almost nine hundred miles away!"

"He's an adventurer," Hastings said. "Had his nose out the car window almost the whole time. That's what I meant

when I said you might not need a new kennel. I think you should just take him with you on your business trips. He's totally comfortable with the motel experience."

"I've always thought Bigfoot hated being in the car," I said.

"Let him ride in the front passenger seat. I must also tell you that we did not address him by the name 'Bigfoot.' We felt his thoughtful personality deserved something more appropriate, and we eventually settled on 'Boswell.' It suits him nicely."

"Does this mean I am his version of Dr. Johnson?"

"That will be part of your own discovery process," Hastings said, closing the photo album. He stood up and reached across the table to shake my hand. "It's been my pleasure," he said.

"What are you going to do now?" I asked.

"Just go slow," he said. "It's difficult without my wife. Very sad. But my sadness has led me to develop a most unexpected affection for country-and-western music. I'm currently taking lessons on the steel guitar."

Before I could respond, a car horn sounded. There were three short honks, a pause, then three more honks.

"Oh, that's his signal," said Hastings. "We'd better wrap this up now so that you can run along."

"My dog is honking for me?" I asked, somewhat uneasily. "Did you teach him that?"

"He learned it on his own," Hastings said, opening the office door and stepping outside. "Remember," he said as I walked past him, "don't be a stranger. Come back and see me whenever you have the time. You're always welcome. Always."

I hesitated, and he could tell I was a bit flustered.

"Don't worry," he said, smiling for the first time. "He's a very capable fellow. You're going to have some wonderful times."

"I'll . . . I will call you," I said. "We'll talk more."

"By all means." He waved, stepped back inside, and closed the door. Then it opened again, and his head poked out. "I should alert you," he said, "that Boswell does get somewhat testy at red lights, and in slow traffic. I think it's a sign of his advancing years. Keep it in mind, though."

"Thank you," I said. The horn honked again, with three short bursts. I began walking toward the car. As I rounded the corner of the building, the horn began a long continuous blast, and the sound got louder and louder with each step I took.

More Bad News for Men

I should've known it was a setup. Why else would such a gorgeous girl look twice at a chump like me? I was just finishing a beer after work when she stopped at my table and said, "You all alone?" God, what a body. Her jeans looked like they were painted on to the most slender, sensuous backside ever created. She noticed me staring that way and smiled.

"How about some lap time?" she purred, and before I could even nod, her sleek posterior was descending toward my receptive loins. Then I heard the sound of my own voice screaming in sudden agony, and everything went dark.

I woke up in a hospital bed and saw a doctor peering intently at massive bruises that covered my upper thighs. The livid purple stains reminded me of newly created ethnic enclaves somewhere in the Balkans.

"Nice going, pal," said a man in a trenchcoat who was standing beside the doctor. "You just got BOSed."

"Say what?!"

"That woman who sat on your lap. She had 'Buns of Steel.' You're lucky you didn't end up in the morgue."

"He's not kidding," said the doctor. "This is Detective Washburn from the Fourth Precinct. I called him as soon as I got your pants off in the emergency room. In cases like this, it's crucial that a field interview be conducted immediately."

"You didn't know the girl, did you?" said Washburn, taking out a small pad of paper.

"No," I said, trying not to groan from the pain. "She, she just looked so pretty. What did you say she did to me?"

"Haven't you seen those workout videos the gals are buying? There's a whole slew on the market right now, all showing how to tighten up their backside muscles."

"However," added the doctor, "new research from the National Institutes of Health and the President's Council on Physical Fitness has shown that, in some cases, the female gluteus maximus can be strengthened to such an extent that its basic physical structure will indeed closely resemble the molecular configuration of various metallic alloys."

"And when that happens," said Washburn, "you end up with a derriere as dangerous as a clenched fist in a brass glove. These BOS incidents are being reported all over the city."

"But why?" I wondered. "What did I do to deserve this?"

Washburn shrugged. "It seems to be a radical feminist form of protest against males in general, intended to discourage us from engaging in what they call 'visual oppression.' Ogling, to you and me."

"I don't suppose you can give us a description of the girl?" asked the doctor.

"Well," I said, "uh, I guess I didn't really notice her, uh, her facial features."

"Because you were looking at her buns of steel," said Washburn. The two of them exchanged a knowing glance.

"We're not blaming you," said the doctor. "All the victims are confused. But right now we don't even know if we're up against an angry loner or an army of the night. That's what makes this whole BOS outbreak so disturbing."

"I wonder," I said, "if this is a crime problem or a public health issue."

"Good point," replied the doctor, "and further complicated by the fact that we're dealing with aesthetic values concerning human anatomy, which are being promulgated through a popular form of mass media entertainment. So you can bet the National Endowment for the Arts will jump in with both feet once the debate starts!"

"Get ready," Washburn said, "for big changes in male-female interactions. No more slap and tickle around the water cooler."

"How long before I get out of here?" I asked.

"Maybe a week," the doctor said. "Be glad you're not the guy two doors down the hall. President of a Fortune 500 company. He was working with a temp yesterday and asked her to join him on the executive sofa for some dictation. BOSed to within an inch of his life. He'll never walk upright again."

The doctor excused himself and said he was going to check on the injured executive. Detective Washburn put away his pen and paper, rubbed his chin, and sighed.

"I guess you should know, your wife's pretty upset about this," he said. "We called her after they got you stabilized in the E-R."

"She's probably filing for a divorce."

"Nah," he said. "She's downstairs in the lobby right now. Wants to see ya. That's the good news."

"What's the bad news?"

"She's with Geraldo Rivera. I gotta tell ya, honestly, the guy looks great for everything he's been through."

"Wait'll he gets BOSed," I snapped.

"That reminds me," Washburn said. "If ya wanna protect yourself from having this happen again, you should get some slacks like the ones I'm wearing. Feel this."

He took my hand and ran it up and down his right leg. "Some kind of polyester blend?" I said.

"Hardly," he grinned. "Super hi-tech kevlar fabric. Completely bulletproof with high-impact absorption."

He reached into a shoulder holster and handed me his Glock 9mm. semi-automatic service pistol.

"Go ahead," he said, stepping back and slapping his thighs. "Remember to hold your breath when you squeeze the trigger."

I got off two quick shots and watched in amazement as Washburn casually dusted off his pants and retrieved the spent cartridges from the floor.

"Nice, huh?" he said. "Stuff was developed for the Belgian Special Forces. Civilian styles are only available by mail-order under a joint venture agreement between *Jane's Defense Weekly* and the Peterman Catalogue."

The doctor suddenly raced back into the room. "What was that noise?" he said, alarmed.

"Just me and my pants," the detective said as he slipped the Glock back into its holster.

A nurse poked her head through the doorway and said, "Doctor! They need you in emergency. Stat! It looks like another one of . . . you know," and she nodded toward me.

"So much for your fifteen minutes of fame," Washburn snorted, and the two of them dashed away. The nurse came over and covered my legs with a bedsheet.

"If you need anything," she said, "just push the 'call' button." Then, very businesslike, she raised the safety bars so I wouldn't fall from the bed. When she turned to go, her white-clad rear end inadvertently brushed against the metal tubing, and I heard the distinct clank of steel hitting steel. She just looked at me, smiled, and winked.

End of the Road

I peered out a grimy window through my binoculars and spotted our prey at the gas station across the street. He was working on a battered sedan in the service bay, completely unaware that his capture was just moments away.

"We're going in!" I snapped. "He's alone. The boss just went to lunch. Now comes . . . endgame!"

"Professor, are you sure we're doing the right thing?" asked Gina, my beautiful graduate assistant. I could tell she was wavering from the strain of our long investigative ordeal.

"Baby," I said, "you've stuck with me right down the line. You know it has to be this way."

"But kidnapping an innocent person— I just feel like there's got to be some other solution."

"Gina, this is too important for the niceties of due process. It's like when the Israelis plucked Eichmann out of Argentina. I've spent most of my professional life researching this guy. It's taken us nine months of legwork to locate him. And there's only two weeks of my current sabbatical left. If he finds out we're onto him, he'll be off like a shot. And he's not an innocent bystander. He's . . . something else."

She came over to the window and kneeled beside me. It was an incredible stroke of luck that our grim little motel was located so close to our objective. "Look at him," I said to Gina, and right then he walked out from the service bay. Instinctively, we ducked lower. He looked around, smiled, then rubbed his forehead with a rag. And he held the rag in a fearsome steel hook.

"You won't be smiling when I get done with you, crab-boy," I hissed. "This time you're not dealing with some teen-agers necking in a parked car."

"Can it really be him?" Gina said. "My God, that story used to terrify me on girl scout campouts. The way the kids heard about the escaped maniac on the car radio, drove away, and then found the hook hanging on the car-door handle when they got home."

"No doubt about it," I said. "He's the ultimate source for all of those bizarre urban legends. The lady who came back from Mexico with the funny-looking dog that turned out to be a big sewer rat? I'm certain she bought it from him! He used to hang around those border towns. And remember the woman with the beehive hairdo who got stung by the spider living in her hair? He was working at a styling salon when that happened! Oh, I'll make him tell us everything, and we'll finally know the real stories behind all these troubling rumors once and for all!"

We had trained for the 'pickup' so carefully that it went off without a hitch. Gina drove the car into the gas station and stopped at one of the pumps. While she feigned indeci-sion over which grade of gasoline to put in the tank, I jumped Hookman from behind. In 12 seconds, I had his mouth gagged and his arms and legs bound with duct tape, and then we tossed him onto the back seat without injury or outside interference. I slipped behind the wheel, and we pulled out of the station. My heart was pounding, and then Gina looked toward the back seat and screamed.

"He's gone! He's not back there anymore!"

"What?!" I was dumbfounded. Trying not to panic, I slowly pulled into the motel parking lot, stopped the engine, and looked for myself. There was no one on the back seat.

"Sweet bleeding Jesus!" I hopped out of the driver's seat and yanked open the back door. Incredibly, our captive had managed to squeeze himself almost completely under the passenger seat, so as to be nearly invisible to anyone in the front of the car.

"A goddam contortionist!" I said. "I should've known. That must be how he pulled off the 'vanishing hitchhiker' routine. Some poor sucker picks him up along the road, and then he burrows under the seat and the driver thinks he's disappeared into thin air!"

"I wouldn't have believed it if I hadn't seen it," Gina said, shocked. "That's one I'll tell my grandchildren about."

"No, don't!" I said. "You'll probably get the details wrong, and this episode will mutate into a brand new legend. Tell the grandkids to read my book, the one I'm going to write when this is over. I'll get a Pulitzer for sure. Too bad the Hugo awards don't have a non-fiction category."

No one saw us carrying our cumbersome load into the room. I had given the motel manager a hefty tip to keep the other units in his disagreeable inn vacant during our stay. I didn't want anyone eavesdropping or interrupting the interrogation process.

We propped Hookman upright on a chair that we had nailed to the floor in a corner of the room. I had also set up an array of tripods that held photographic lights, still cameras, and video recorders, so the entire procedure would be fully documented.

Gina started the videocams rolling as I yanked the piece of tape from Hookman's mouth. "Are you a cop?" he snarled. "Am I under arrest for something?"

"I'm not a cop," I said, "I'm a professor of sociology. And you're not under arrest, although God knows I'm more than fully qualified to have that kind of power."

"Damn, it stinks in here!" he said. "What the hell do you want from me, anyway?"

I looked around the room. He was right, it did reek of filth. There were soiled clothes lying on the floor and greasy paper bags stuffed with fast-food leftovers piled high in the wastebaskets. It looked like a battle zone, I thought, and then I turned back to the sneering prisoner.

"I want answers, pretty boy," I said, grabbing him roughly by the collar on his coveralls. "And don't think you're gonna scare me with that claw or pull your disappearing act again."

"How did you find me?" he demanded.

"Well, that's better," I said, turning to Gina with a smile. "You see?" I said. "He knows we're onto him!" I turned back to Hookman. "I had access to all the information resources of a major university," I said. "It took hundreds of interviews, and thousands of hours combing through newspaper files and wire service reports of strange incidents. A babysitter terrorized by someone calling from the upstairs phone. Puppies and kittens blown up in microwave ovens. Little by little, though, I picked up vital clues. You thought you'd covered your tracks, but you never figured someone like me would come along. Now you're gonna talk."

"You can't make me do anything." His smugness was maddening.

"Oh, but I can," I said. "There are no Geneva Convention rules here. I have lots of tricks to loosen your tongue."

"Why should you even care?" he asked. "Can't you leave well enough alone?"

"Attitudes like that are destroying this country!" I said. "These offbeat tales drift through our national consciousness, diverting our attention from truly important issues like deficit reduction, and sapping the collective mental energy we should be using to debate national health care and the future of social security. But all that will change once I've exposed you!"

I leaned in, examining his face from just inches away.

"What are you?" I asked. "An alien being walking our planet for eternity, sowing fear and suspicion? Or is this some government plot to keep us all distracted while our individual liberties are slowly eroded by the unseen power elite?"

"Maybe there's more than just me," he said with a tight smile. "Maybe there's a whole family. Anyway, you'll die wondering."

"Gina," I said, "make him sweat for a while. Keep the hot lights in his face while I go search his apartment."

Hookman fixed me with a look of surprise and malice.

"Oh yes," I said. "We know where you live. We've been following you everywhere. I'm sure I'll find lots of good stuff."

I fumbled through his pockets and came up with a set of keys. He didn't struggle. It seemed like his resistance might be ebbing.

"Don't give him any water, nothing," I said. Gina nodded.

His apartment was tidy and seemed perfectly normal. However, on the floor of the bedroom closet I found a thick scrapbook. Inside were dozens of old, yellowed newspaper clippings. Some of them described the same strange incidents I had been studying for years. But others told of incidents that I had never heard about during my research.

It was like striking gold, and it was all the confirmation I needed. I put the scrapbook back in the closet, figuring I would have plenty of opportunities to come back later for a more thorough examination. I couldn't have been more wrong.

When I got back to the motel and opened the door to our room, the chair in the corner was empty. "What the. . .?!" I blurted. Looking around, I saw rolls of filming on the floor, exposed. Video cassettes were smashed and broken open, the tape strewn in all directions. I examined the damage slowly, totally stunned. Then Gina appeared in the doorway, looking drained.

"It's over, professor," she said. "Done. Finished."

"What the hell's going on here?" I said, enraged. "How could you let this happen? What'd he do to you?"

"We had a long, serious discussion about life and the nature of reality. But it doesn't really matter what he told me," she answered. "This is about you, not him."

"You're not serious. Tell me this is a sick joke."

"And you're not the man I knew when we first met. You've become obsessed. I should have said something earlier, months ago, when my feelings started to change. But it's hard for a student to accept the fact that her teacher is on the wrong path. Look at yourself. Your hygiene is terrible, your skin is blotchy. And this—" She poked a finger between my lips and wiggled one of my teeth, and I tasted my own blood.

"You're even showing early signs of scurvy because your diet is so bad. How could you not notice?"

"Look, maybe things aren't as good as they used to be," I said. "But even if that's true, is it all my fault?"

"Not really," she said. "Mostly I blame the tenure system. Permanent job security and lack of peer review have turned you into an amoral, irresponsible glory-seeker.

"Did it ever occur to you that we all need a bit of mystery and intrigue in our lives? The telling and re-telling of these urban legends is part of our cultural communication process, a unique outlet for the collective anxiety and suspicion that builds up in every well-developed society. We shouldn't tamper with it."

"So, now what?" I asked. "What do I tell the department chair when we get back to school?"

"That's your problem. I'm not going back."

"Not going back? What about the Ph.D.? You're so close!"

"Not anymore. I'm dropping sociology, professor. You've wrecked it for me. I didn't want to tell you until I was absolutely sure, and now I am. I've been accepted into the M.B.A. program at Harvard. Good-bye, professor. I'm sorry."

There was nothing I could say. A taxi pulled up outside the motel a few minutes later and took Gina out of my life. When I went back to Hookman's apartment, it was stripped clean.

These days, I teach my graduate seminars and try not to think about what might have been. Sometimes I wonder what my nemesis is doing out in the real world. He's on guard now, so I'm sure no one will ever get close to him again. But I know he's thinking about me.

Nice Work If You
Can Get It

The interview was held in a cramped, stuffy old office on the third floor of National City police headquarters. The room felt steamy in the summer heat, and the air was filled with wisps of stale cigarette smoke. Three men were seated behind a long steel desk. They rose to greet me as I entered. Their faces were shiny with perspiration, and all of them looked tired.

"Thanks for coming in," said the man in the middle, whose bushy black hair was so disheveled that it appeared to be trying to escape from his head. "I'm Jim Blundell."

"Pleased to meet you, Mayor Blundell," I said, shaking hands. On his right was a tall, muscular fellow wearing a dark blue uniform.

"This is Carlton Sulley, chief of police," said the mayor, nodding toward the big man, "and over here is Sid Wigstrom, city manager." Wigstrom had thin, birdlike facial features and wore thick horn-rimmed glasses. We exchanged greetings and sat down.

"I'm sorry if this seems rushed," said the mayor. "We've had a lot of applicants and not much time. We hope to have the interviews wrapped up today so that the person selected can be introduced next week during our 4th of July parade."

"That sounds exciting," I said, trying to establish some positive connection with the trio.

"As you know," said the mayor, looking at some papers on the desk, "we're looking for someone to replace ElectroFlame. He's gone over to Capitol City and taken over for the Emerald Ranger, who has retired. Now, I've got your resume here, so I just want to confirm some of the information. Has Captain Frost always been your alter ego?"

"Yes, sir," I said, "right from my first case."

"And you've been based in Middletown for the past five years?"

"Correct. Started there after I graduated college."

"Let me ask you this," said Wigstrom, the city manager. "Why did you decide to be a superhero?" He leaned forward in his chair as he spoke, and peered intently through the thick lenses.

"Well," I said, "I've always enjoyed helping people, and it seemed like an exciting life . . . besides my, you know, power."

"You didn't have any relatives killed by criminals or anything like that?"

"Not really," I said. "I did have a cousin who was once seriously mauled by a dog."

"The reason I ask," said Wigstrom, "is that we've found the most dedicated crime fighters are the ones who have had some direct criminal experience in their background. The others seem to get soft after a while."

"Oh, that wouldn't be a problem," I said emphatically. "I don't have any sympathy for criminals."

"Middletown isn't a very big city," the mayor said. "What's the population there, fifty- or sixty-thousand?"

"About that," I said.

"We're close to eight-hundred-thousand here," the mayor said. "That's a big step up, don't you think?"

"The quest for justice knows no limits, city or otherwise," I said. I wasn't sure what it meant, but I thought it sounded determined and forceful.

"What's your other identity like?" asked the police chief. "You going to have any trouble finding a job?"

"That shouldn't be a problem," I said. "My family owns a chain of tire stores, so I have lots of work experience mounting and balancing. But I don't have to bother with that, frankly. I have an ample trust fund."

"Better watch that," said the chief. "Crooks are always on the lookout for people with big bank accounts. Be nice if you could be a regular citizen, just to avoid suspicion."

"How will we summon you when we need your help?" the mayor asked. "Do you have a distinctive signal? Flare gun?"

"I use a remote-controlled thermometer," I said, pulling the thin glass tube from a secret pocket in my vest. "When you flip a switch on the special transmitter, the mercury in this thing rises into the danger zone. Then I'm alerted."

"What do you plan to use for transportation?" the chief asked, unwrapping a stick of chewing gum and lazily shoving it into his pudgy mouth.

"A high-performance motorcycle," I said. "It handles just about any kind of terrain."

"You've never been downtown here at rush hour," the chief replied coolly, snapping the gum as he chewed. "That could get real interesting. ElectroFlame had a nice rocket belt."

"I, um, don't do well in high places," I admitted. "Problem with my inner ear." The room fell silent. Wigstrom drummed his fingers on the table. The mayor cleared his throat.

136

"I think," he said, "this would be a good time to give us a demonstration of your power. What could we use for a test?"

"How about your coffee cup?" I suggested. "Is there anything in it right now?"

"Half full," he said, raising the cup to his mouth for a sip. "And lukewarm. Story of my life."

"Okay, put the cup out on the middle of the desk," I instructed. I rubbed my hands together and then held them out with the palms facing down and my fingers pointing toward the cup. In a few seconds a beam of bluish light shot out of my fingertips and bathed the coffee cup in an eerie glow. A moment later I relaxed and the beam faded. The mayor picked up the cup and turned it upside down. Nothing spilled out.

"Frozen solid," he said, and handed the cup to Wigstrom. "So, you make things cold. What else?"

"That's about it," I said.

"Can't warm it back up?" the chief asked.

"No, it doesn't work in reverse." I sensed a perfunctory tone creeping into their questions. The mayor made some notation on a pad of paper.

"Does this mean," Wigstrom said, rubbing his chin thoughtfully, "that your body can withstand tremendously cold temperatures? Like, if a super-criminal tried to freeze *you*, what would happen?"

"Hmmm," I said, momentarily taken aback. "Well, to be honest, I guess I have no idea."

"No idea?" Wigstrom repeated quickly, sounding irritated. "Haven't you ever tested out that possibility? Been curious about it?"

"It just, um, it's never come up," I said. "How would I test that, anyway?"

"Just ask your local butcher if you can spend a few hours in the meat locker," the police chief suggested.

"That might work," I agreed. "But I am a vegetarian." There was another long silence. The chief leaned back in his chair and let out a long sigh. The mayor made another notation on his pad of paper.

"So, how'd you get this power?" Wigstrom finally asked. "Did you recite a magic formula? Drink some chemical?"

"I think I was just born with it," I said. "I didn't even really notice it until I started going through puberty."

"Tell me this," said the police chief. "What do you think *causes* crime? Have you ever wondered about that?"

"Oh, I suppose there are lots of reasons," I said. "Remember Lex Luthor? He was Superboy's friend until Superboy accidentally caused a laboratory accident that made Luthor's hair fall out. So in that case, simply going bald was enough to make a good man turn against society."

"You know, I never really bought into that explanation," said the chief, taking off his hat to reveal a smooth, shiny pate. "I went bald in my twenties, and it was no big deal. I think ol' Lex had a few extra kinks in his hose, so to say."

"Or, more likely, he was just born bad," I suggested.

"Who are some of the criminals you've defeated?" asked the mayor.

"Well," I said, "the Cobra was probably the biggest."

"The Cobra?" He looked puzzled.

"Yes," I said. "He used trained snakes to help commit his robberies. They kept the victims at bay while the Cobra scooped up all the goods."

"Hmm," said the mayor. "I must have missed that one. You fellas know anything about the Cobra?" They shook their heads.

"So how did you handle that case?" the chief asked.

"I caught him in the act, robbing a bank. So I just froze his snakes. Then the security guards jumped on him."

"Froze the snakes!?" Wigstrom said, as if in pain. He clamped his eyes shut and shook his head. "No way," he said, "no, no sir, can't do it, capital-N capital-O."

"We have a very active animal-rights chapter in this city," the mayor explained. "They'd have us in court in two minutes if you pulled a stunt like that here."

"Oh, good point," I said.

"It's always something these days," said the police chief, sounding almost sympathetic. "Makes me nostalgic for World War Two. Nice and simple then. Us and the enemy. Electro-Flame was just a kid, but he was chasing down spies and saboteurs faster than we could fingerprint 'em! And the only thing in this town worth blowing up was the grain silo!"

"Look, Captain Frost," said the mayor. "I'll be honest. You have good credentials, but this is a major metropolitan area. We've got several candidates with far more experience than you. IronFist, The Human Bullet, and Megaman are ready to step up to this level. I'm afraid you're not. But I appreciate your time, and I'd like to give you a voucher that's good for a free sandwich of your choice at Dinah's Roto-Chick on Main Street."

"Oh, that's not necessary," I said. "My mother packed me a lunch for this trip."

"You be sure to thank her when you get home," said the chief. He seemed to be trying to stifle a smirk.

They asked me to send in the next applicant on my way out. I was startled when I walked through the waiting room and saw a buxom blonde wearing a shimmering red nylon body suit and a blue cowl over her face. A large yellow 'S' curved between her breasts, an 'E' covered her tummy, and an 'X' was suggestively positioned on her crotch.

"Wow!" I said. "Who are you?"

"Passion Girl," she answered in a provocative tone.

"Where are you based? That name isn't familiar."

"Actually," she said, "this would be my first gig."

"You're kidding! Nobody starts out in a city this big. What's your power, anyway?"

She just smiled coyly and walked past me toward the interview room.

*   *   *

On the way home I stopped for gas and a soda at a dusty little two-pump station. A portable TV set was propped on a chair near the service bay, blaring out dialogue from a soap opera. The grimy attendant stared at the screen from a distance as he filled my tank.

I was walking to the restroom when a familiar figure rounded a corner and almost bumped into me. It was Megaman.

"How you doing, kid?" he asked.

"I bombed. Not enough experience. But I heard you're on the short list."

"Not anymore," he said, holding up his portable phone. "The mayor called me about an hour ago. Said they were hiring some broad. I thought I'd seen it all, but this is a new low."

Right then, the little TV set began to emit a strange squawking noise, and the picture faded out. Megaman started toward the set and motioned for me to follow. "Someone's taking control of the airwaves," he said.

As we watched, a new image on the screen came into focus. It was a man's face, grinning with maniacal glee. He had a green complexion and a third eye in his forehead.

"Occupants of National City!" he cried. "You are my slaves! I, Kalgalor, am collecting you for my trophy room! In moments you will all be residing in *this*, your new home!" He held up a large glass bottle, the kind you see on water coolers.

"He's going to shrink all of us!" I said, my voice quivering slightly.

"Hang on, kid," Megaman said calmly, and then he called to the attendant, who was inserting coins into a candy machine. "Hey, buddy! Are we inside the city limits?"

"No way," said the attendant, not bothering to look away from the machine. He was trying to decide whether to purchase a Zagnut or an Abba Zabba bar. "City line is a couple of miles back down the highway," he added.

"That's what I thought," said Megaman. Then, turning to me, he said, "Watch this, kid. It should be interesting."

In a moment the telephone poles that lined each side of the highway began to rock back and forth and the wires bounced wildly up and down.

"He's really doing it," Megaman said. "When the power poles in the city shrink, they start pulling everything else in that direction. Like reeling in a fishing line."

The portable phone started ringing again. Megaman put it up to his ear. "Hello? Yes. Oh, that's very interesting. An hour ago I was chopped liver. Uh-huh, I know what's going on. Well, I need some time to think it over. Thanks for calling."

He hooked the phone back onto his belt and rolled his eyes. "That was Mayor Blundell. He said, 'Save us and the job's yours.' Can you believe the nerve?"

"You're going to do it, aren't you?" I said. "I mean, you're not scared of that green villain?"

"Kalgalor? He's just an impish prankster from another dimension. All I have to do is trick him into saying his own name backwards, and he's automatically thrown back into his own world. But if you ask me, the best thing that could happen to that city is to spend a couple of months brooding quietly at the bottom of a 20-gallon jar."

The violent rocking motion of the telephone poles began to settle down. The TV screen was now dark and silent.

"Well," said Megaman, "I have my pride, but I also have a career to think about." He ran behind the station and a moment later I heard a loud humming sound. It was Megaman's distinctive turbo-jet ultralight helicopter. It suddenly rose into view, swung out over my head, and landed a few feet away.

"You can come along if you want!" Megaman yelled over the sound of the engine. "This could be your big break. Maybe I could bring you on as my assistant."

"No," I said, "I'll get another chance someday. Right now there are more important things in my life I have to deal with."

"Yeah? Like what?"

"Well, as soon as I get home, I'm going to pack up all the stuff in my room and start looking for my own apartment."

Megaman smiled knowingly. "Nice going, Captain. You're doing the right thing." He gave a thumbs-up sign and revved the engine. The chopper lifted off and hovered above me for a few seconds.

"Wish me luck, kid!" he called out. "See ya in the funny papers!"

The little aircraft sped away with a roar. And just before it disappeared from view I thrust one fist up to the sky. "Yes!" I shouted. "Yes, you will!"

Olympic Combined

"Oh my, it's a beautiful morning, just perfect for these opening ceremonies. And, Keith, I believe that's the team from Andorra leading the way now. A very tiny country with a big athletic spirit."

"Actually, Jim, that's the band from Alcorn State. With the Games switching over to this new, totally open format, many people think the battle for musical supremacy will be one of the highlights of the entire schedule. Alcorn takes on Pearl Jam later today and has a good shot at the medal round if they get some winning momentum."

"Keith, here comes a real surprise. The Secretary-General's Trophy goes to Canada for this entry, entitled 'Drops That Spot.' It's a whimsical look at the acid-rain controversy, with more than thirty-thousand red and white carnations used to construct the long border on this massive three-dimensional map.

"The entire display is just over seventy-five feet long, and the Canadian team members are swimming in a miniature dead lake that was made from five hundred gallons of real meringue."

"Certainly a credit to our northern neighbors, Jim. And amid the competition, there is also cooperation. Here's a combined entry from Poland, Slovenia, and the Czech Republic called 'Who Needs Vowels?' The huge figures of well-known Sesame Street characters Bert, Ernie, and Big Bird appear through the courtesy of the Children's Television Workshop, and they are shown playfully bashing the unwanted letters with huge lollipop sledgehammers."

"Keith, a lot of action is going on at the judging platform, so let's check with Dick and Peggy for the latest."

"Jim, Peggy and I have just been watching the Royal Lipizzan stallions give an awesome display of moonwalking to the accompaniment of Michael Jackson's hit tune 'Beat It.' The horses are each outfitted in jet-black polyester jumpsuits with matching wraparound sunglasses. Peggy, what d'you think?"

"Dick, I really believe this was a breakthrough for the stallions in terms of style, athleticism, and choreography. They were getting excellent height on the jumps, and their gestures were wonderfully interpretive."

"Oh yes, the hoof movements—so subtle and yet definitive. And the silver hoof covers—absolutely stunning."

"Dick, here come the scores now, and they aren't very good, either. This is not going to make the riding school happy. A couple of five-twos, a five-one, even a four-nine, my goodness!"

"Well, that's the judge from the Dress Barn, and she's been very hard on all the entries using synthetic fabrics, so we shouldn't be too surprised. I hear there's more excitement at the starting gate, so let's go back to Keith."

"Thanks, Dick, it's a historic moment here. The first-ever appearance by a team from Vatican City. Their entry is called 'Urbi et Orbi,' which we're told sort of means 'Here, There, and Everywhere,' and it features two dozen life-size replicas of famous church personalities, including the Emperor Constantine, Thomas à Becket, Archbishop Fulton Sheen, and Charlton Heston. At the controls is Giovanni Cardinal De

Cordova, who is the focus of some controversy. Jim, what about that?"

"Keith, it's the old bugaboo—experience. De Cordova hasn't had much international competition, and some of the other participants felt he didn't have the skills to drive here."

"Ah, and here's what the Games are all about, Jim—a team with just one member. I believe this is the Republic of Vanuatu, represented by Ilekai Kulandani, and he's carrying a handsome ceremonial shield from his homeland."

"No, Keith, that's Homer Formby. Furniture refinishing is one of the demonstration events this year, and Homer should take the gold easily. He's holding a beautifully handcrafted Colonial breakfast table that required only light sanding and a thin coat of oil stain to bring out the natural wood lustre."

"Oh, Jim, look at this! Vatican City is off the course! They're up on the sidewalk, didn't even make the first turn, and that means immediate disqualification! What a blow this will be to their whole program!"

"Keith, we said it earlier: Cardinal De Cordova is not an experienced driver, he wasn't familiar with this route, and he obviously hit that turn much too fast. Now it looks like he's spinning himself into a rut down there."

"Jim, I think this would be a perfect time to remind our viewers that some emergency services for today's festivities are being provided by Bulldog Brothers Towing, in exchange for the following promotional announcement. We'll be right back."

This Means War

BEAVERTON—A Sunset High School student remained hospitalized Friday with burns suffered when he and a companion packed a fresh turkey full of black powder and tried to blow it up. Fire department investigators said it was a home science experiment and the boys were trying to simulate a nuclear explosion.

—*The Oregonian*, March 1990

We were screaming across enemy territory at treetop level in order to avoid detection by radar when I looked over and saw my co-pilot weeping quietly into a bowl of freshly cut salad greens.

"Lieutenant Baker!" I yelled, and he looked up just in time to feel the palm of my hand strike his cheek smartly.

"Sorry, Skipper," he said, "I just never thought it would come down to this."

"None of us did," I pointed out. "But we've all got a job to do, and yours is getting those greens prepped so that the molecular structure remains compatible with the other components. If you can't handle it, I'll get someone else up here. You copy?"

"Aye aye, sir."

I watched as he reached beneath his seat and inserted a plastic security clearance card into the coded lockbox that contained all the necessary ingredients for a deliciously smooth yogurt and poppyseed dressing, lightly seasoned with a subtle blend of garlic, paprika, and Uranium 238.

My mouth began to water as I thought about the enormous energy field that would soon be constrained only by the thin lead-lined walls of a simple Tupperware bowl balanced on a man's lap. But there wasn't time to brood about the consequences because I suddenly heard a crackling in my headphone.

"Bombardier to bridge!" It was the shrill voice of Lieutenant Powell, and I could tell instantly that he was upset. "Skipper, we got trouble back here!"

"On my way," I snapped.

The passageway to the rear of the plane led me past the navigator's post. In that cramped cubicle, Captain Angelo Creamora was carefully adjusting the flame on a compact gas stove while stirring the contents of a gleaming stainless steel Revereware saucepan. He and I had been friends longer than anyone else in the crew, ever since our early days at flight school when we both volunteered for the culinary wing.

"Checkin' up on me?" he said, winking.

I leaned over, and the warm aroma of freshly simmering stock drifted up to my nose.

"Back the flame off just a hair," I said. "We're not at high altitude anymore."

He grinned sardonically. "Jim," he said, "*you* back off, okay? It's just turkey parts."

"Captain, I'm giving you a direct order!" The coldness in my voice brought me up straight. How could I treat my best buddy like that? "Creamy, I'm sorry," I said quickly, dropping the formality of rank, and he nodded with understanding.

"You know what's at stake here," I said. "We both saw the pictures from the test sites." He nodded again, grimly this time.

During those top-secret experiments, it was demonstrated with graphic, horrifying clarity that when the ingredients of a traditional American holiday dinner were vaporized and then dispersed in a symmetrical pattern with atomic force, the most extensive damage was caused by the impact of highly energized giblet particles traveling at nearly the speed of light.

"Make sure that doesn't reach maximum kinetic potential until we're almost to the drop zone," I cautioned.

"Isn't there a chance this could be just another drill?" he asked.

"I don't think so. On the drills, we always get a high-frequency radio pulse that's fed directly into the onboard microwave system and activates the 'slow defrost' mode. This time, the signal went straight to the convection oven and started the 'quickbroil' cycle. Looks like we're really serving this one up."

"Damn," he said. "I suppose I only have you to blame for all this." I nodded silently. Creamy was one of the few people who knew that I was the single most important person involved in the conception and execution of Project Butterball.

It had all begun years earlier, during a casual outdoor family barbecue. I was reclining in my favorite lounge chair waiting for the coals to heat up, when I stumbled upon some critically important information in an obscure publication called *International Cooking Policy Quarterly*. What caught my attention was a short article by Julia Child entitled "Thermonuclear Options After the First Course."

"There's one thing I've always wondered," said Creamy. "How did this all stay secret for so long?"

"Because the people who knew about it were very, very careful," I said. "There's a trait that's common to almost any person who spends a lot of time in the kitchen. Something strange happens to the human mind when it becomes fascinated by the process of stimulating the palate and ritualizing the preparation and consumption of food. A code of silence binds people with this type of personality, a kind of nutritional 'Omerta.' It's almost impossible for an outsider to break through."

"So how'd you do it?" he asked.

"We rounded them up one by one," I said. "Sometimes it got ugly."

I remembered one particularly brutal interrogation of James Beard. It took nearly ninety hours of force-feeding him Crisco sandwiches and Jujubes before he revealed the formula for a concoction he called Mutual Assured Destruction Bread Pudding.

And then there was Peg Bracken. She had memorized the entire manuscript of an unpublished autobiographical tome entitled *The I-Hate-To-Cook-and-I'll-Blow-Your-Whole-Country-Away-To-Pro ve-It Book.* I'm not proud of what we did to Peg, but we got what we needed. Years later I heard that she had made a partial recovery and was dabbling in custards, and Tang.

"Who would believe it!" said Creamy. "To think that some of our most cherished entrees would become instruments of mass destruction. God, we're a perverse society!"

"Don't whip yourself too much," I said. "Almost every civilization throughout history has known that certain animal proteins become highly unstable in the presence of specific complex carbohydrates. All you have to do is combine them in the proper sequence and you've got Armageddon on the half-shell."

"You're telling me that other cultures have possessed this kind of power?" Creamy was so surprised he almost dropped the stirring rod into the saucepan.

"Our research found numerous examples of well-known catastrophic incidents that have previously been explained as naturally occurring events, but which were, in fact, elaborate mass feedings that somehow went out of control."

"Such as?"

"The destruction of Pompeii. It wasn't a volcanic eruption. Core samples from the area, re-examined with our most advanced carbon-dating techniques, showed unmistakable traces of an early form of Veal Scallopini spread over the entire blast zone."

Creamy's eyes narrowed as the implications sunk in.

"The hell with it!" he said, finally. "Let's just get this mission over with. How's everybody else doing?"

"Not great," I said. "Baker is having trouble up in the cockpit. If he can't handle the yogurt dressing, I may need you to whip together a simple vinaigrette."

"Just give me the word," he said.

"Skipper, where are you?!" Lieutenant Powell sounded frantic on the intercom. I moved on toward the payload preparation compartment.

When the twin doors slid open, I was almost flung backward by a chorus of invective emanating from my three weapons specialists, all of whom were hunched over a long steam table where the Big Bird was resting in a shallow pan. Lieutenant Powell was flanked by Sergeants Ernie Hays and Bobby Lambert, and they were obviously frustrated and angry. The bird itself looked tender but not overly juicy, which concerned me immediately.

"What's the problem?" I queried.

"Look at this," said Powell, holding out a familiar instrument. "The goddam baster is kaput. See here? A hairline crack in the bulb. Means we have no suction capacity, zero. How do you like that? Damn thing costs six-hundred dollars, too. I coulda picked one up at Thriftway for sixty-nine cents before we left."

"Don't panic," I said. Reaching into my jacket pocket, I slowly withdrew a slim, lightweight carrying case covered with a handsome simulated-hickory-wood finish. Inside was a sterling silver basting kit, complete with mint-scented Handi-Wipes for easy cleanup. Powell took the case in his hands, looked almost reverently at the barrel of the basting wand, saw the inscription that had been expertly engraved years before, and then read it out loud for the others.

"To my friend Jim. Mi Hibachi es su Hibachi. Forever Yours, Graham Kerr."

"You knew the Galloping Gourmet?" Hays asked, his voice trembling. "I used to watch that show every day. My mom would fix me a glass of milk and a plate of Ding Dongs."

Suddenly the fuselage rocked with a tremendous impact and we were all thrown to the floor. When I looked up, there was a small hole in the side of the compartment and air was rushing out.

"What the hell was that?" yelled Powell. I jumped to my feet and inspected the damage up close.

"Some kind of missile," Sergeant Lambert said, but I knew different.

"Don't be too sure about that," I said, pointing to several tiny, smoldering chunks that were imbedded in the metal siding of the plane. I tasted one. "Just as I suspected. A standard weight pork loin. Probably shoulder-launched. Anti-

Soviet guerrilla fighters developed them in   Afghanistan. We're lucky it didn't cut us in half."

"It might as well have done!" Hays shouted. "That hole is where the bread locker used to be! We just lost the entire supply of biscuits!" I could feel panic in the air.

"Sergeant Hays," I said calmly, "you'll prepare a substitute starch immediately. Go to the cockpit and tell Lieutenant Baker to give you all the croutons he can spare from the salad. Call me on the headset when you're done."

Luckily the bird was still resting undisturbed on the steam table. Powell was already using my commemorative baster with cool-headed efficiency. His unflappable nature was the result of a long family involvement with hot, oily liquids, the details of which I have never been able to pin down.

"Hurry this up!" I said. "We need to begin the loading sequence before anything else goes wrong! How's dessert coming?"

"Mocha almond torte with thirteen layers of cobalt-blueberry filling," said Lambert. "Mom always said my pastries had a half-life of two-hundred years."

"Fine," I said. "Has anyone heard from Major Kelly in the bomb bay?"

"He popped in just before you showed up," Powell replied. "Said he was gonna be double-checking the drop coordinates."

"I'll make sure of that," I said. It took less than a minute for me to climb down the ladder that connected the payload prep compartment to the loading bay.

As I straightened up and turned around, I saw that Major Kelly was busily decorating the massive steel bomb casing with a series of homoerotic photographs by Robert Mapplethorpe. He looked at me defensively.

"Isn't this what we're *really* fighting for?" he asked.

Before I could answer, the plane shuddered again, and I could feel the g-forces pushing against me as we began to climb steeply.

"Commander to co-pilot!" I yelled into the intercom. "Baker, what're you doing up there?"

"I just received a code-red abort message on my transponder link, skipper! Says we should turn back immediately!"

"I'm getting it too, Commander," said Lieutenant Powell. "All my temperature controls just went dead and the auto-lock mechanism sealed up the oven door. This bird isn't going anywhere."

By the time I got back to my seat in the cockpit, Baker had received priority-1 confirmation that we had been scrubbed.

"They claim it was all a software glitch," he said. "Told me to hightail it out of here and they'd explain everything when we got back. I hope we don't run into company along the way."

Sergeant Hays was crouched behind Baker's seat. The pockets on his flak vest were stuffed with croutons, and he was holding the salad bowl tightly with both hands. "Thank heaven it was all a mistake," he said. "Skipper, you think we'll get home in time for dinner?"

I suddenly remembered that the base menu had listed kidney stew with sweetbreads as the main course that evening. It occurred to me that if God really existed, he certainly had a flair for ironic details.

"Bogeys on the radar, skipper," Baker said. "They're closing in on us."

"Hold on, boys," I said, pushing out the throttle. "If I can get into some cover, we'll be slicker than syrup on a short stack." I was aiming for a giant swath of cumulus clouds that were billowing up on our left.

"That's a good strategy," said Hays. "How 'bout that great big one there?" He pointed to one of the puffy white orbs looming above the rest.

"That looks like a giant dumpling," Baker said.

"Dumplings have great mouth feel," Hays said. "Don't you think so, skipper?"

I didn't answer. I wished at that moment that the entire world could be bland as steamed rice and uncontested as mashed potatoes. I wished that people like Lieutenant Baker and Sergeant Hays and the wife I should not have divorced could all roll together in luscious layers of smooth parfait and sleep on beds of warm shortcake, without worrying about fire and death raining out of the sky.

"This whole business gives me heartburn" is what I said, and then nobody talked again for a long time.

Spooked

The doorbell rang at precisely 4:30 in the afternoon. Through the peephole I could see little Tommy Warren standing on the porch. He was dressed in a Superman costume and was carrying a small briefcase.

"Well now," I said, opening the door, "are you trying to get a head start on the other goblins? It's still early."

Tommy didn't smile. "I'm having some friends over for a party in one hour," he said, "so I only have time for a couple of house calls." Then he stepped inside and closed the door.

"May I see the goods now, sir?" he asked.

"Beg pardon?"

"The candy," he said. "What are you giving out this year?"

"I'm not exactly sure," I said. "My wife takes care of that, and she's out at the moment. Would you care to wait here while I check in the kitchen?"

"I think it would be better if I came along," he said. The tone of his voice was vaguely confrontational.

There were three plastic bags of candy on the kitchen table. "Here we go," I said. "Looks like we have Snickers, Milky Way, and Almond Joy 'fun size' bars. I guess I should put everything into a big bowl, eh?"

"That won't be necessary."

"Beg pardon?"

Tommy eased himself into one of the chairs at the table and placed the briefcase beside the candy. "Please have a seat," he instructed, and as I complied he made a careful examination of each bag. "I'm glad you opted for a quality product," he said. "I hate gross homemade stuff, like popcorn balls."

"Well, we try to keep the customers happy around here." Something about the situation was making me edgy. I realized that I wanted Tommy to leave, and soon. "Shall we open these up and you can be on your way?"

"No hurry," he said. "Now, I am stating for the record that these bags are still sealed from the factory. Do you have any problems with that?"

"Um, I don't think so."

"Good," Tommy said. "That simplifies things." He took a legal-size piece of paper and a ballpoint pen from the briefcase and placed them on the table between us.

"What I am proposing," he said, "is a simple binding agreement. Recognizing that you have not yet opened the candy, I will release you from any and all liability that may result from my becoming ill, maimed, or otherwise incapacitated as a result of eating said candy within a period of 180 days from this date."

"You want *all* of it?"

"Everything," he said. "You'll be indemnified against any potential claims by me on the sole condition that all three bags are delivered into my possession at the end of this meeting."

"Tommy," I said slowly, "what grade are you in?"

"Fifth."

"Is that where these ideas originated?"

"Yes," he said, "in my Law and American Society class."

"I didn't know that was part of the curriculum at John Adams."

"Oh, I'm not at John Adams anymore," he said. "Our district went to a voucher system this year, so I enrolled in a special private academy. It's awesome. I'm even learning how to access the Internet."

"I see. Well, how do you think other kids would feel if you got all of my candy? Then nobody else could trick or treat here."

"I'm glad you brought that up," he said, "because I've done some research. Your front porch, for example, has a bottom step that is several inches higher than code allows."

"I'm aware of that. The front walkway has settled over the years. It's not uncommon with older houses."

"It still poses a significant risk of personal injury, especially for young children wearing bulky costumes on a dark night. Limiting your exposure to that risk is in your best interest, and you can do that by limiting the foot traffic up and down the steps tonight.

"Once I'm in possession of the candy, you simply remove the pumpkins and other decorations from the porch, turn off the lights, and you're home free. It's a mutually beneficial outcome."

The telephone rang just then. When I picked up the receiver, a woman's voice began speaking in quick staccato sentences.

"This is Tommy's mother. I'm on my car phone. Don't say a word until I'm finished. I know he's in there because I'm secretly following him, and I want to make sure he isn't intimidating our neighbors with a bunch of legal mumbo jumbo. He doesn't mean any harm, but he's just been in a litigious mood lately. Try to negotiate with him. If that doesn't work, you can feel free to kick his little behind out the door, in a nurturing manner if at all possible."

"Is that so?" I said, playing along with the ruse. "Well, I appreciate the call, but I don't think I'll subscribe at this time. I have strong moral objections to your swimsuit issue."

I hung up the phone and noticed that my camera was within easy reach on top of the refrigerator.

"Tommy," I said, "I want to get a picture of that great costume." Before he could say anything, I snapped off two quick shots. "Did you make it yourself?"

"Not exactly. My mom sewed it for me. Do you suppose we could get back to the agreement now?"

"Absolutely," I said. "Although, as a responsible adult, I should first confirm that you and your mother followed the proper procedures regarding trademark and copyright arrangements for the Superman character?"

He looked startled. "What do you mean?"

"I mean you have a lot of potential liability of your own riding on that big red S. Remember how much trouble Mr. Skanky had down at the magic shop when he painted Bart Simpson's face on the front window? The Fox Network almost put him out of business."

"But why would I get in trouble?"

"Wearing the costume to obtain candy means you are securing material benefits through the use of a property that is licensed and controlled by DC Comics. I wouldn't mess with those folks."

"How would they even know?" Tommy asked, sounding a bit nervous for the first time.

"Because of this, remember?" And I held up the camera. "I believe the proper term is 'Exhibit A.'"

We compromised. Tommy got three fun size bars of his choice and agreed to close off the discussion immediately. As we stood on the front porch, he was clearly chagrined.

"Hey, don't fret about it," I said gently. "Sometimes Halloween pranks can backfire. When I was your age, I got hauled into the principal's office for spraying Burma Shave in my teacher's favorite hat."

"What's Burma Shave?"

"Ask somebody on the Internet."

"You know," he said, "next year I may just skip the candy and collect for UNICEF. My parents said it'll look good on my record when I apply to college. You should think about how much you'll want to contribute."

"I'll do that."

"Actually," he went on, sounding more assertive, "I don't have to be home right away. Maybe I'll stop next door and see what kind of deal I can work out with Mrs. Wackenhut."

"Frankly, Tommy, I wouldn't bother if I were you."

"Why not? Is she a lawyer?"

"Worse than that," I said. "She's giving out popcorn balls."

Megathon

DAY 1: As I join the other entrants at the starting line on the warm sands of Zuma Beach, I look down at my legs and am awed by their virile sensuality. For a moment it seems as if I have been training for this moment all my life, meticulously empowering myself for the incredible ordeal that lies ahead.

"Wait, don't move," says Emile, my support-team captain, as he reaches toward my face. There's a glint of silver in his hand and I hear a metallic click. "Got it," he says, smiling. "You had a giant, rogue nose hair growing out of your left nostril. I could see it from here. That would've looked really bad on TV."

The starter's pistol cracks and we bolt for the surf to begin the swimming portion of the competition. I am leading the pack when someone's elbow hits my chest. Staggered, I look over in time to see the smiling face of participatory sports journalist George Plimpton, aged but still undaunted, as he cuts in front of me.

His aggressive strategy backfires when Plimpton trips over a long electrical cord that is attached to a microphone cradled in the hands of Hawaiian crooner Don Ho, who has set up his act on the beach to serenade us with a musical send-off. Sprung free, I splash into the waves, while Plimpton is buried under a human pileup and the air is filled with a combination of angry shouts and the lilting melody of "Tiny Bubbles."

DAY 3: Trouble arises during the urban-equestrian portion of the race, when my purebred Appaloosa gelding, Xenophon, throws a shoe as we gallop through the intersection of Sunset Boulevard and La Brea Avenue.

I quickly dismount and begin leading my steed toward the nearest aid station, when we unexpectedly wander into a crowd that has gathered along the Hollywood walk of fame to celebrate the dedication of a new star honoring the late paragon of movie western sidekicks, Gabby Hayes.

The sight of my limping horse galvanizes veteran actors James Drury and Robert Conrad, both of whom rush to assist me. Using their knowledge of ranching lore, they re-attach the iron shoe using only a pen knife and some old toothpicks. Conrad also performs an invigorating Oriental Trail Massage on Xenophon's neck and shoulders, and I reach into my back pocket for a rule book to confirm that such assistance is allowed.

"Don't worry about that," Drury says. "No laws or regulations of any kind are enforced here. This area was recently declared a federal enterprise zone."

DAY 8: Paddling my kayak northward off the coast of Big Sur, I pause to rest my shoulders and reach for a drink when a sneaker wave washes the plastic beverage bottle overboard. Efforts to retrieve it are interrupted by the ringing of the cellular phone inside a waterproof Gore-tex pouch strapped to my left thigh.

"Don't ingest any more of your sports drink!" commands the voice of Emile. "The manufacturer just admitted that it contains a synthetic enzyme that has been shown to cause abnormal thyroid enlargement in lab tests on male ferrets. The story is airing right now on CNN. I'll meet you at the next checkpoint and we'll switch over to Sunny Delight."

"Thanks," I respond tiredly. "But what do you suggest I do when I get thirsty?"

"As soon as I hang up, take the battery out of the cell phone and suck on it, as if it were a pebble. Weren't you ever in the Boy Scouts?"

DAY 16: Knee deep in Oregon's MacKenzie River, I have no time to gloat over the hefty scores I've racked up in roller blading, ballroom dancing, and automotive trouble-shooting. Flyfishing is not one of my strong events, and the river is very cold.

Reeling in what I believe to be a good-sized bass, it turns out I have tangled up someone else's line. Just then I hear heavy splashing footsteps heading toward me. In the next instant I am face to face with angling legend Grits Gresham, purple with rage. He grabs the tangled lines out of my hand and gives me a violent shove backward into the swiftly moving water.

Miles down river, I crawl ashore exhausted and bleeding from numerous bumps and scrapes. With darkness falling, I hear a distant pounding noise and begin walking toward it. My hopes rise further when I spot the glow of a campfire ahead.

In the flickering light I can see men with painted faces beating drums and chanting, and believe I may have found one of the Northwest's native tribal communities. But when I enter the clearing and fall to my knees, I find myself looking up into the steely eyes of poet Robert Bly and I realize I have interrupted a backwoods male consciousness-raising seminar.

DAY 19: Bly and his band have restored me to health but refuse to let me leave without undergoing a ceremonial purification of my masculine spirit. By the light of a full moon, we march to a remote hillside where Bly points toward a small cave.

"Enter," he says, "and do not come out until you have confronted the beast inside, the man-beast that lives within us all. Conquer him and free your soul!"

Just then I hear a low moaning sound coming from the cave, and chills tingle up and down my spine.

"Is there really a wild creature in there?" I ask.

Bly leans close to my ear and whispers, "Don't worry, it's just Salman Rushdie."

DAY 20: Emile is frantic when I reach the next checkpoint. "Where have you been?" he demands, handing me a pair of leather pants and matching jacket for the upcoming motocross segment. "The cocoa futures market collapsed yesterday! I couldn't unload your shares without authorization, so your portfolio has lost half its value and you're dead last in personal finance."

When I explain where I've been, he brightens a bit. "I'll get a signed affidavit from Bly," he says, "and we can count that as a wilderness experience, which is on the list of optional events. It should balance out your fiscal point losses."

I gun the cycle's engine as he hands me a sheet of paper listing all the competitors. "You're still in the top five," Emile says, "but I just got word that former Olympic gold medalist Bruce Jenner has scored a perfect 10 in the swimsuit competition, so he's on a record pace right now."

DAY 27: I'm making good time during the hitchhiking event. My new best buddy, Atlas LeRoy McErvin, picked me up outside Detroit in his bright red Kenmore. I am treating him to lunch in a diner at the 'Manila John' Basilone Memorial rest stop along Route 80 in Pennsylvania when a news bulletin flashes on a TV set behind the counter.

The announcer reveals that Bruce Jenner is out of the competition, stricken by infectious hepatitis after having himself tied to a cross and lowered into a vat of industrial effluent during the performance art segment of the race. Atlas is alarmed.

"I gave that bum a ride from Milwaukee to Dearborn!" he exclaims. Fearing contamination, my buddy spends the next few hours on the road, endlessly repeating the Lord's Prayer and various song lyrics from *Jesus Christ Superstar*, a soul-numbing reverie that does not end until we reach New York City and I spot a storefront clinic where he is able to obtain a gamma globulin shot.

DAY 33: Sitting backstage in the auditorium of P.S. 119 in Brooklyn, Emile applies a light powder under my eyes while shaking his head with disapproval. "Your skin is ravaged," he says. "You haven't been applying moisturizer between checkpoints."

"Spare me the lecture," I reply. "Where do we stand?"

"You still trail Plimpton by a slight margin. He's trying for a knockout blow in tonight's stage presentation segment by renting the Masonic Hall in Queens, where he will produce, direct, and star in the entire six-hour version of *Nicholas Nickleby.*"

"Good grief! Do you think he can pull it off?"

"I was getting to that." Emile grins. "I've just received word that he lost his voice after the first 90 minutes, so he'll need to lip sync the rest of the show. It'll cost him a lot of style points, but he's still going to score high on audacity."

Encouraged, I proceed onstage for my own theatrical effort and hold the audience spellbound with an original one-man adaptation of the famous Reader's Digest article, "I Am Joe's Pituitary."

DAY 35: My worst nightmare has come true. Plimpton and I are in a virtual tie going into the final event.

My feet feel like lead weights as I pound my way up the stairs of the Empire State Building. I try to inspire myself with thoughts of the Sea World blimp *Shamu*, which is moored at the top floor observation deck, waiting to carry the winner off to an all-expenses-paid vacation in south Florida. Plimpton, however, matches me step for step. With just a few flights to go, I begin to hear his heavy breathing over my shoulder.

Then, on the landing of the 89th floor, my right knee collapses. The pain is excruciating. Grabbing a hand rail for support, I feel someone rush past me. Looking down at my knee, I see blood oozing out and realize I've been hit with a blunt object. A few feet away, Plimpton lies unconcious on the stairs below. Bathed in sweat and gasping, I stagger on and finally reach the door to the observation deck, flinging it open with a shout. But there is no one waiting to greet me, no ESPN anchors, nothing.

Gazing skyward, I see that *Shamu* has cast off its mooring cables and is drifting out over Manhattan with all the race officials and other dignitaries onboard.

Fireworks explode in the sky. Automobile horns are honking in the streets below. The whole city is celebrating the finish of this Herculean contest.

My cellular phone rings, and when I put it to my ear Emile is yelling frantically. "Someone jumped on the express elevator and got to the finish line ahead of you! I'm trying to call the judges, but the switchboard is jammed!"

I drop the phone and realize I am about to pass out. Squinting into the distance, I see the electronic message board begin flashing along the underside of the blimp. Just before I slide into blissful oblivion, I am able to make out the words, "Congratulations Tonya Harding."

Make It Count

Read these instructions carefully before you begin. If you do not follow correct procedures, your vote may not be properly recorded.

First, make sure the door to the booth is fully closed and the security bolt is in place. The bolt activates a set of warning lights outside the booth to guarantee privacy. You should see a neon glow through the small pane of safety glass in the upper-right-hand corner of the door.

Once you have secured the booth, take a moment to look around and familiarize yourself with its features. Every effort has been made to insure that your participation in this election will be a pleasant and comfortable experience.

May we make a suggestion? Many voters find that last-minute deliberations are highly stressful. Before starting, you might want to head for the basin at the far end of the counter and freshen up a bit. Towels and washcloths are in the drawers underneath. Also, the voting machines are extremely sensitive to contamination by dirt or small particulates, so it's very important that your hands be thoroughly clean.

Are you in a hurry? Don't be. Decisions made in haste are soon regretted. If you are here on your lunch hour, we have a complete menu available—everything from light garden-fresh salads to hearty full-course main dishes. (All the selections are listed in Appendix A of this voters' pamphlet.) When you are ready to place your order, simply push the "Call" button next to the light switch on the intercom panel.

When you want to start the voting procedure, please be seated at the workstation and face the video screen. Place your hands flat on either side of the keyboard and breathe deeply for ten to fifteen seconds. You should feel relaxed and confident. If you are too warm, do not hesitate to loosen your garments, or remove them completely. The small fan above the workstation can be activated and adjusted by using the remote-control pedals located under the desk.

This system uses the new LANDSLIDE software program, which was developed specifically for electoral purposes. It is virtually foolproof. However, if you should make an error or become confused after you have begun voting, simply pick up the red telephone beside the terminal and dial the toll-free number listed on the mouthpiece. A technician will assist you as soon as one is available.

While you are waiting, a variety of audio recordings are available for your listening pleasure on twelve separate channels. A guidebook containing the complete listing for each channel is enclosed in the large manila envelope taped to the back of your chair, along with dialing instructions. We have made every effort to bring these recordings into compliance with the latest statutes governing bilingual voting materials.

If you feel you need more time to deliberate the initiatives and consider the candidates involved in this election, pull down the small viewing screen mounted above the washbasin. This will activate a short instructional film, *Your Mark in History*, narrated by Fess Parker, which demonstrates the importance of individual voters in American politics. Headphones will drop from an overhead rack. These are disposable, and should be placed in the wastebasket at the conclusion of the film, or you may keep them as a souvenir of your visit.

When you have finished voting, be sure to ask the precinct captain for a rating card and fill it out before leaving. We cannot improve service if we don't hear from you. By filling out the card, you also automatically become eligible to win our Election Sweepstakes. Watch on Inauguration Day—you may hear your name announced on national TV by the new Chief Executive!

Now the rest is up to you. Medical technicians and life-saving equipment are standing by in case of emergency.

If you are ready to begin, press the "Start" button on the keyboard in front of the video screen. And thank you for not smoking.

Meeting of Minds

"Well then," said Miss Stafford, "in conclusion I must say your daughter is one of the brightest first graders I've ever taught. Arianna is cooperative, never exaggerates the extent of her own quite considerable intelligence, and always displays a very positive attitude about classroom activities."

I smiled at my wife, Viveca, who was beaming with pride. Had any parent-teacher conference in history ever been more satisfying? It was especially rewarding to hear such compliments from Miss Stafford, a prim and somewhat stuffy woman in her early forties who was rumored to be extremely dubious about the parenting skills of modern American adults.

"Thank you," I said. "We do think she's quite special."

"Before we adjourn, there *is* one thing I need to ask you about," Miss Stafford said, reaching up to adjust her thick horn-rimmed glasses while staring down at the note pad on her lap. The tone of her voice suddenly had an edge to it. The bun of hair on top of her head seemed to grow tighter.

"Now, Mr. Butterbury," she continued, "could you please tell me, as briefly as possible, what exactly is . . . MJ-12?"

There was moment of silence before my wife said, "Oh God!" in a gasping whisper. She clapped both hands to her face and closed her eyes. The air in the room felt heavy.

"I'm sorry," said Miss Stafford, "I didn't mean to startle anyone."

"Oh, don't apologize," I said. "I'm just, I mean, we didn't expect that question. Where did you hear about, er, this particular subject?"

"From Arianna," Miss Stafford said. "Here, look. She made this drawing a few weeks ago."

She handed us a piece of thick, cream-colored paper. In green crayon, there was a crude sketch of three aerial disks flying above a house. Each disk was clearly labeled 'MJ-12.'

"I've talked to her about it privately," said Miss Stafford. "Apparently it has something to do with unidentified flying objects. She says you know all about it."

"This is, um, kind of awkward," I said, handing the drawing back to Miss Stafford. "What we're dealing with here is, well, MJ-12 is an abbreviation. It stands for Majestic-12."

"Which is—?"

"It's . . . " I looked again at Viveca, who had closed her eyes and was shaking her head.

"Supposedly," I continued, "MJ-12 was a select working group of high government officials that was formed to investigate the crash of a flying saucer back in 1947."

"Oh, I see," Miss Stafford said casually, scribbling in her notebook. "Is this something she saw on *The X-Files?*"

"No," I said, feeling flustered. "She, well, she went into our bedroom and found some of my UFO books recently." I was trying not to sound defensive. "I keep them on a special shelf. And, since she can read at fourth-grade level, she quickly got the gist of the whole subject and started quizzing me about it. I decided it was better to just tell her what I know."

"Wise decision," Miss Stafford agreed. "It's hard to keep secrets with kids around. And you can't prevent them from talking about what they've learned. So, where *was* this crash?"

"People claim," I said, "that it happened near the town of Roswell, New Mexico. But nothing has ever been proven. The wreckage was supposedly taken to Wright-Patterson Air Base in Ohio for analysis."

"I can't listen to this!" my wife said abruptly. "I should have made you throw that trash away years ago! Why can't you be interested in something more normal, like fly fishing?"

"Oh dear. Let's cool down here for a minute," Miss Stafford said, closing her notebook and standing up. "I'll get us some drinks and we can have a calm, productive discussion."

She walked to a small refrigerator on a shelf in a corner of the room. "All I have is mango-pineapple swirl," she said. "It's only fifty-percent real juice, but it's not too sweet and it has a really crisp, clean aftertaste."

"That sounds fine," I said. Viveca just nodded.

"I can tell you're nervous," Miss Stafford said as she poured the swirl into paper cups. "And it doesn't help that I have a reputation for being a stick-in-the-mud," she added.

"Oh, I don't think that's true," I lied instantly.

"Sure it is," she said, handing each of us a cup. "Mr. Butterbury, school is the ultimate information superhighway, and I'm standing in the middle lane. When one of my students pokes around the basement at home and finds a stack of old *Playboy* magazines or a dead cat or a few sticks of dynamite, I hear about it."

"Dynamite?" said Viveca. "You're kidding!"

"Absolutely not," said Miss Stafford. "Family life in this country is quite amazing. For example, there's at least one student at our school whose father is wearing women's undergarments right now. So, compared to other situations, this UFO thing with Arianna is pretty harmless. Now, I know a little bit about flying saucers, but MJ-12 is a new spin. You say the government formed a group of experts to study a crashed object?"

"Right," I said. "Supposedly there was wreckage, alien bodies, the whole nine yards."

"And is this group still in existence?"

"Well, nobody really knows. It was top secret."

"Hmmm. Then how does anybody even know about MJ-12?" she asked. "See, I'm trying to get a handle on where this information is circulating. That would help me predict how soon other kids may pick up on it. Obviously, it hasn't made the cover of *People* magazine yet. So how did the whole thing start?"

"Some official documents," I said, "or, rather, copies of official documents were sent anonymously to a UFO researcher a few years ago. And people have been arguing about their authenticity ever since. It's all very controversial."

"He also subscribes to a goofball newsletter, if that's what you're wondering," Viveca interjected, dryly. "Crop circle updates, all that nonsense. And he listens to a strange talk show every Thursday night on shortwave radio."

"You're the third parent in the past six months who's mentioned shortwave radio," Miss Stafford said, making another note on her papers. "I may have to get one, just so I can tap into that medium if the need arises."

"I'd be glad to sell you ours," Viveca said.

"I can tell by your tone that you aren't very compelled by any of these offbeat topics," Miss Stafford said.

"It just seems terribly silly," Viveca said. "I've gotten used to it, though. This is a man who can hardly remember his own birthday, but he's memorized huge blocks of dialogue from old *Star Trek* episodes. Now that's a *real* mystery."

"But I'm careful to monitor what Arianna watches," I said. "My folks were a little too lax in that regard, I'm afraid."

"I think we've pretty much covered everything we need to in this matter," Miss Stafford said. "From what you've told me, I have the feeling that MJ-12 is not being actively debated within your household."

"No, never," said Viveca decisively.

"In that case, I suspect Arianna may not even bring it up again. Although, once she's old enough to start dating, you'll probably wish she was more interested in UFOs."

Viveca looked at her watch. "I need to call home and tell our babysitter we're running late," she said, sounding more than a bit irritated. "Can I use the phone in the main office?"

"Oh, absolutely," said Miss Stafford. Viveca hurried out the door without looking back. I stood up and suddenly felt my undershirt soaked with perspiration.

"Tell me something," Miss Stafford said. "How do you feel about that flying saucer stuff? Honestly?"

"Well," I said, "if they really exist it's probably better that society doesn't know. It would just cause a big uproar. Look what happened with that whole 'cold fusion' fiasco."

"True enough. And I appreciate your candor, Mr. Butterbury. As I said, Arianna has probably forgotten about it. Just don't be surprised if she stumbles onto something else you've tried to keep hidden away."

"Well," I said, "I'd better be going too. I'm very happy that my daughter is doing so well. Thank you, again."

"You're welcome," Miss Stafford said. We stood up and shook hands. When I reached the door, she said, "Oh, Mr. Butterbury. There's one thing I forgot to tell you."

I stopped and looked back. Miss Stafford raised her right hand with the second and third fingers spread apart in a perfect Vulcan salute. "Live long and prosper," she said.

You Name It

". . . So it looks as though current conditions will put Hurricane Alice onshore sometime tomorrow morning. Back to you, Norm."

"Thanks, Jim. While Alice is wreaking havoc along the Southern seaboard, people out West are having a different kind of trouble. Kate is in our newsroom with more."

"Well, Norm, city officials in Los Angeles say Earthquake Bob did a lot more damage than first reported. It could be the worst shaker since Big Hal rumbled across the San Fernando Valley two years ago."

"Thanks, Kate. A quick note here. Emergency crews in Northern California say Mud Slide Vivian should be totally cleaned up in the next day or so. She's been blocking roads in two states since heavy rains and swollen rivers sent her fearsome gooey power crashing out of the hills last week. Now let's check with Rita in the chopper."

"Norm, I'm just east of the I-5 bypass, right above the awesome aftermath of Train Wreck Smitty. Looks like two freights met head-on this morning. Investigators think Smitty could be a real bear if any of those tank cars rupture and release dangerous chemicals."

"Stay on top of it, Rita. Of course, we can't talk about Smitty without thinking back to last year, when Toxic Cloud LaJean crept over the East Side on Thanksgiving night. Experts are still baffled by her sudden terrifying appearance in that sleeping neighborhood. I'm told we now have a special report coming in from David at the mall."

"That's right, Norm. Police here have just announced the existence of Bomb Scare George. No word on the likelihood of George being upgraded, but all patrons are being urged to leave the mall immediately. Officials don't want a repeat of what happened at the Shoreline Center two summers ago, when several shoppers were slightly injured by Mystery Blast Roxanne."

"David, we'll certainly check back with you if time allows. This has been a rough day for air-quality managers. Linda is in Mobile One to explain why."

"Norm, two million drivers headed to work this morning, and right now Smog Alert Walter is chuckling all the way through the afternoon commute. Heavy smoke drifting in from Brushfire Josephine is adding to the problem, so keep those headlights turned on for the ride home."

"Sound advice, Linda. And while there's no need to panic on the freeways, a lot of investors are panicked in the wake of Bank Collapse Jethro. Two more arrests made in that case today, and our consumer expert, Melvin, is at the Hall of Justice."

"No real surprises here, Norm. The two suspects are huddling with their lawyers. But the big news is a possible break in Product Tampering Helen, where, three years back, tainted corn pads caused severe foot problems. We are told that a suspect will be in custody by the week's end."

"Super job, Melvin, kudos all around on that one. Let's go upstairs now and see what Larry is working on for Late-Cast."

"Norm, Detroit is planning new marketing incentives to perk up sales after the embarrassment of Recall Elvin. We'll

WANDA

FRED

BONNIE

WALLY

RITA

have details. City Hall has decided to go ahead and pay for repairs at Memorial Auditorium after that building was nearly torn apart by the sudden fury of Rock Concert Riot Midge. And, hard to believe, but the Tall Towers Power Plant is all set to glow again, just six months after Meltdown Manny sent thousands fleeing."

"Norm? Norm? This is Linda again. I hate to interrupt, but we've got a breaker here in Mobile One, and it looks big. The signal's pretty garbled, but we know it's Doc Gorman checking in from over at Westmeadow. Boy, all the bells are going off on this one."

"We're holding, Linda. This sounds like a toughie."

"Yes. The static is clearing, Norm, and—oh-oh. Seems like we're getting a recurrence of Anomie Bette, up on Grape Blossom Drive. At first glance, this seemed like the initial stirrings of Anomie Cecil, only the local experts are telling us it's the same old Bette we thought we'd seen the last of late on Friday afternoon. She's on a circular path, I guess, but the downside is that she's paired up with Nameless Dread Wilhelm."

"Linda, can you tell us where this double-barreled attack has hit? Do we have any focus on that yet?"

"Affirmative, Norm. Even as we speak, crisis units are arriving at the home of Fred C. Burch, out at 35228 Grape Blossom. We'll speed to that address and try for a live update later this evening."

"Is that Person Fred, Linda?"

"You got it, Norm."

'Tis the Season

I could feel a surge of family pride rising among our little group gathered around the tree in the living room as my adopted brother, Timor, finished a medley of holiday classics.

His strong, throaty voice had alternately cooed and cajoled its way through the emotional nuances of "The Little Drummer Boy," then raised the tempo with a moog-synthesized update of "Jingle Bell Rock" before segueing effortlessly into an extended disco version of "A Horse With No Name."

Applause filled the room, and I felt a hand on my shoulder. From behind me, Auntie Cluster leaned close and said, "Josh, your idea of adding karaoke to our celebration this year was sheer genius. I just wish I could figure out what's causing that odd, pungent odor in here."

"Dexter," I said, pointing toward the far corner, where my nephew was operating the sound equipment. "He told me it was some kind of lubricant for the control board. A likely story."

"Oh my," she said. "I hope it's not another quack remedy he's using for that pesky dander problem of his." She paused, and then added, "Could you hand me a glass of water? I'm getting very dry."

As I watched, she emptied the glass onto a thick, bushy corsage handcrafted from cuttings of Ponderosa pine and *Ilex vomitoria* that had unexpectedly taken root in the moist, humus-like folds of her baggy shetland wool sweater.

"I was going to plant this thing in the back yard after dinner," she whispered, "but I got a call today from NHK Network in Japan. They want to come and film it next week."

Before I could respond, Uncle Elmore stepped into the room and motioned for me to follow him. He walked quickly into the den, where Grandma Gommy was already waiting, and closed the door.

"Something incredible has come up," Elmore said. "I was seeing to the turkey, and while I was poking around with the baster I discovered tiny excavations in the dressing. They seemed to indicate the presence of an entire, miniature civilization! I believe it's evolving right now, even as we speak!"

"Bother!" Gommy exclaimed. "I *knew* we should have had ham!"

"Let's not panic," Elmore said. "It's only 5:30. We need to come up with a plan."

"How far along are these people?" I asked.

"Hard to say," Elmore replied. "The terracing may be evidence of a planned development, and I think they've started to master advertising. I saw a tiny billboard that said 'If You Lived Here, You'd Be Home by Now.'"

"Shouldn't we tell Dad?" I asked.

"Goodness no!" Gommy gasped. "You know how much he hates those ticky-tacky housing projects!"

At that moment, Auntie Cluster opened the door and poked her head inside. "What's going on here?" she asked in a low voice. Although her hair and the adjoining foliage of the corsage obscured my view, I could see Timor standing in the hall behind her.

Elmore beckoned them both inside and explained the situation. "Do you think we should call someone?" Aunty Cluster asked. "The 9-1-1 people might know what to do."

"This is out of their league," Elmore said. "I was thinking of calling Stephen Jay Gould."

"The dinosaur man?" Gommy said. "That sounds promising but," and she rubbed her hands together somewhat anxiously, "you *do* know he's Jewish?"

"Of course I know," Elmore said, "which means he probably doesn't have anything else going on tonight. Am I wrong?"

Timor looked at me and said, "It's your turn out there. To sing."

"Josh," said Auntie Cluster, "let's you and me perform a duet." She grabbed my arm and pulled me toward the door. "Can you remember all the words to 'Whiter Shade of Pale'?"

In the hallway we were suddenly confronted by my twin cousins, Earl and Sandy. They were holding a leather strap attached to a small object that was quivering under a foamy coating of purple froth. When I noticed two little brown eyes staring up at me, I realized it was our sainted Pomeranian, Ramses II.

"I gave them permission to flock the dog," Auntie Cluster said. "It was the only way to get them out of the kitchen."

As we passed the doorway of the library, a voice called out. Our next-door neighbor, Niles, and his wife, Emerald-Plaza, were standing beside the Franklin stove holding a plate of hors d'oeuvres.

"C'mere and try this," Niles said, holding out a small cracker coated with a cheesy substance. I bit into it and tasted a hint of rosemary.

"My latest invention," Niles said, reaching down and picking up a bulbous, sausage-like item wrapped in cellophane. "I call it the all-purpose cocktail log. Spreadable, great for snacks, or. . ."

He swung open the little door on the stove and tossed the tube inside, where it burst into multi-colored flames.

"Goes for about three hours," he said, grinning. "Smells great, too."

"Have you heard about what's going on with the turkey?" Emerald-Plaza asked. News travels fast in our house.

"Doesn't it sound amazing?" Auntie Cluster said. "Perhaps the little civilization will show us new things, unlock ways to conquer diseases, and help us find lasting peace."

"Well," said Emerald-Plaza sourly, looking at her watch, "they better do it by six o'clock, because that's when you people said we'd be having dinner, and I'm famished."

I turned to go out but accidentally opened the wrong door and found myself staring into a small closet. A precarious stack of large, round, black objects loomed in the darkness.

"What are all these tires doing in here?" I asked.

"Josh, shame on you!" Auntie Cluster scolded. "Those are gourmet, imported after-dinner mints! I was going to surprise everyone."

"My God, they're heavy," I said, trying to lift one. "Are they solid chocolate?"

"No, they're filled with marzipan. Come away from there right now!"

She and I never did get to sing our duet. I heard a commotion in the dining room, and when we got there everyone was talking excitedly about Uncle Elmore, who had abruptly grabbed the turkey from the oven and left. But then, as if on cue, Dad appeared and told us all to sit down at the table. When everyone was settled in, he went back into the kitchen and returned with a second plump and fully cooked bird, steaming on a magnificent Wedgewood platter.

Sitting down beside me, he winked and casually slipped a copy of the hardbound reissued commemorative edition of the 1929 Johnson-Smith joke catalogue onto my lap. Sensing a plot, I opened the volume, and right there on page 341 was a detailed drawing of a gag item called The Evolutionary Turkey.

"Newly available," Dad whispered. "It's rigged to explode into a snowstorm of confetti in about an hour." He chuckled. "I just couldn't put up with another year of Elmore sitting here showing us how he learned to eat with his toes in New Guinea."

As we were joining hands to say the blessing, the doorbell rang. Timor went to check it out, and came back a few moments later, looking alarmed. "It's Mr. Gould!" he hissed. "He says someone left a message on his answering machine to get right over here. What should I do?"

"Ask him to join us," Dad said. "He can sit in Elmore's place."

"Darling, that's a true gesture of the season," Grandma Gommy said. Then, considering it further, she added, "And thank goodness we're not having ham!"

Curtain Call

An era ended early this morning when the last comedy club in America closed its doors for good. Harry's Slap-Shtick Shack was a fixture in San Francisco's North Beach district for nearly six decades. It survived the economic battering of two wars, numerous recessions, urban re-zoning, cable TV, and disco, only to be killed off by a combination of changing social values and government good intentions gone amok.

How could this happen in a nation that was once so richly blessed with an abundance of homespun hilarity?

"Simple," said club owner Harry Gleason. "There are no more jokes. They've all been told. No jokes, no audience." Rows of empty chairs surrounding a makeshift wooden stage served as mute testimony to his words.

"He's right," agreed a portly, balding Jay Leno as he stood beside Gleason, surveying the scene. "I ran out of funny material almost ten years ago. It's amazing that Harry's been able to hang on for so long."

It was hoped that a famous name on the marquee would boost the club's anemic attendance figures during its final week of operation. The strategy failed. Leno, like many ex-comedians, has carved out a comfortable niche by working the educational circuit; he now performs mostly at elementary schools. His current act, a blend of wild animal calls, hygiene tips, and contortionism, is popular with pre-teens but has never attracted a mass audience.

"I thought we'd maybe get a couple-dozen people in here tonight for the last show," Gleason said. "The way I feel now, you could knock me over with a featherbed." In fact, the only customers present were two grizzled regulars, who sat slumped over the bar and gave their names as Hardcore and The Beamer.

Both men had spent most of the evening tossing back highballs, and neither even glanced up when Leno stepped to the microphone and announced that he was being released from his contract and would abstain from a final performance.

"No way," Gleason explained afterward, "am I going to demean the heritage of this entertainment form by signing off in front of an empty house. I'd be damned by show-business historians forever. Better I should beat my head against a dead horse."

Leno smiled as he slipped his paycheck into his wallet, but when he spoke there was bitterness in his voice. "This," he said, "is the legacy of the Sonny Bono presidency. And to think we all believed it would be a comic bonanza!"

"I warned you, but nobody would listen," Gleason interjected. "You see, people never stop and think how painful it is to be laughing about something and then realize, 'Oh God, this is no joke, it's *reality!*' And with Sonny running the country, that kind of thing happened so often it completely destroyed the boundaries between comedy and real life. Eventually, folks got thoroughly confused and they just stopped laughing."

"It started a crazy cycle," Leno added. "As more and more citizens turned away from comedy, the notion popped up that we were running short of jokes. That's when Congress jumped in. It should've been obvious right then that we were all doomed."

He was referring, of course, to the ill-fated Humor Protection Act, which many analysts now blame for the persistent cynicism and melancholy attitudes that seem to permeate all levels of American culture.

"What they didn't realize," Gleason said, "is that when you designate a certain type of joke as 'threatened' and place a moratorium on it, the problem only gets worse."

"Look at it this way," said Leno. "If I'm basing a routine on humor about relationships and I see in the paper that in-law jokes are suddenly off limits, my natural impulse is to say, 'Hey, I better cash in on my other material before the government clamps down on that, too!' So comics started using up all their spouse jokes and sibling jokes, and suddenly everybody panicked and comedians started pillaging *all* categories of funny anecdotes. It was a catastrophe for the amusement industry."

"Plus, you can't believe all the permits and paperwork we had to go through," Gleason lamented. "And talk about paranoia—it got so bad you couldn't even laugh at a guy slipping on an icy sidewalk without having a cop in your face screaming, 'Where's the gag, pal?! Who's giving you the funny stuff?!'"

Leno rolled his eyes just thinking about it. "Then the dominoes started falling," he said, "because at that point the joke supply really *was* in trouble. Pretty soon the clubs started to shut down, TV sitcoms went off the air, comic strips folded. We just got trapped in a huge downward spiral."

At this point Hardcore looked up and muttered, "Humor comes and humor goes, but Earth abides."

The Beamer nodded and held up a thick, tattered paperback book. "All this was foretold," he said in a raspy voice.

"The Cold War, global warming, the Tailhook Scandal, all of it here in the teachings of Nostradamus!"

Leno looked at the two men quizzically and said, "They're kidding, right?"

"If we could figure that out, we wouldn't be in this mess," Gleason said ruefully. "Gag me with a chainsaw."

There was no point in lingering. Leno and the two dazed regulars hurried away as Gleason made sure all the lights were turned off. Minutes later, standing outside in a chilly drizzle, he slipped a chain through the handles of the thick glass doors and secured it with a heavy padlock.

"Did I mention that someone wanted my old sign?" he said, pointing up toward the swirling tubes of neon-coated glass that spelled out the club's name in huge block letters, along with the tagline "Laff 'Till Your Butt Aches."

"A guy from the Smithsonian called yesterday and asked if they could have it," Gleason continued. "You know, since it's kind of a cultural artifact. So I told him the new tenants are planning to open a Christian Science reading room, and they want to keep the sign because of its religious significance. Guy didn't even register a chuckle. He just says, 'Oh, okay. Sorry to bother you,' and hangs up."

Gleason stepped onto the sidewalk and thrust his hands into the pockets of his rumpled overcoat. "God, what a weird feeling," he said. He paused and shivered for a moment, and then a look of bemused recognition spread over his face. "I'll be darned," he said. "It feels just like a cold day in Hell!"

He turned and began walking away at a brisk pace. Then his shoulders began to shake noticeably, a distinctive mannerism that could only mean one thing: Harry Gleason was laughing.

Jeffrey Shaffer's humor has appeared in such places as *The New Yorker, Wall Street Journal,* Portland *Oregonian, Seattle Times, Detroit Free Press,* and *Baltimore Sun* Sunday magazines. In addition to writing his humor, Shaffer does humorous radio commentaries for Oregon Public Broadcasting. Shaffer has never done his humor standing up. He lives in Portland, Oregon.

Paul Hoffman has illustrated numerous books for a variety of publishers, including Workman, Running, Rodale, and Harvard Common. For Catbird, he has illustrated Arnold B. Kanter's three volumes of humor about lawyers and the law, most recently *The Ins & Outs of Law Firm Mismanagement.* Hoffman lives in Greenfield, Massachusetts.

If you would like to find out what else Catbird Press publishes — its specialties are prose humor and humorous Central European and American fiction — please write, call, fax, or e-mail us and we'll send you our catalog:

Catbird Press, 16 Windsor Road, North Haven, CT 06473
800-360-2391; fax 203-230-8029; catbird@pipeline.com